The Silence of the Wilting Skin

TLOTLO TSAMAASE

The Silence of the Wilting Skin

TLOTLO TSAMAASE

PINK
NARCISSUS
PRESS

This book is a work of fiction. All the characters and events portrayed in this book are fictitious or are used fictiously, and any resemblance to real people or events is purely coincidental.

THE SILENCE OF THE WILTING SKIN
© 2020 Tlotlo Tsamaase

Cover illustration & design by Duncan Eagleson

Published by Pink Narcissus Press
Massachusetts, USA
pinknarc.com

ISBN: 978-1-939056-17-7
First trade paperback edition: May 2020

To Mama, Papa and Mmêmogolo (for lost days).

My Girlfriend was born on the train a week after her mother died.

"Trust no man without a shadow," my grandmother used to say. "If shadows are felled from their owners it means the body is vacant of a spirit. Something felled them."

We have a train station that no one boards in our wards. It's decrepit and takes its specific passengers to and fro—somewhere. Somewhere no one wants to go. My dead grandfather always has his palm against the window, a silent wave, trying to catch us in our adolescent growth. My still-born brother wavers next to him, slumbering on a hammock-like cushioned chair hanging from the rail. He is grey-skinned with dark-brown eyes so beady with aliveness it pains my heart. There are about five dead in our family and we're still counting. My boyfriend is huddled next to them, holding them. He still carries that quiet expression with him, an expression that has slain itself as a martyr for someone.

I prefer to only see my family dead, for we see them in their true identities. The only time we ever become us is when we're dead; when we're dead we become the still-Black font of sky. My dead family calls the color on them still-Black hoping it will still itself onto our bones. But we don't refer to them as dead to their face, they are still here, they are still a part of us, more than we could ever be

From our window, the fields are a wisp of green, a

railway line stitched across them. We can see it in the distance from our balcony using our telescope. You can't be near the dead without catching their fever.

"The graveyard opens early today," my brother says, walking into the living room with a limp in his left leg. He holds a tray of tea for Grandma. "We should get there early to avoid long queues."

"It's 3:00 a.m.," I say, pushing the telescope down. But we can't ignore the train's horn. It is a wail; its nails drag into the still night.

"That's the perfect time. The night guard will be on his shift and might give us tea, phaphatha and a warm place to hold up in," Brother says.

"I haven't finished knitting this for my brother," I say, lifting an untold fabric. "I will be done in a few hours."

"He is dead," Brother says. "He doesn't actually get the chills. Better give that to Grandma. You know how she can't bear the cold. She wants to get an early night so she's not tired for our visitation in a couple of hours."

"Mxm, whatever, just stop making me feel guilty," I say, clicking my needles against each other as I thread yarn through them.

"The fare has doubled—"

"Again? What the hell. It went up last month. I don't think washing dishes is going to cut it anymore," I say, banging my fist against the table. "And we still have last month's rates to pay."

"If we don't pay, they're just going to relocate our dead relatives to some Satan-worshipping asshole who will make them work menial jobs with dithokolosi."

"Eish, please. Like, you don't need to remind me. We're seeing our grandfather tomorrow! He's going to have questions, and I don't want to lie to his face again this time. I swear they will drag him out the train this time and he'll be slaving around for those evil *things*. And you?

Where's your money?"

"Having a kid is expensive," Brother says, staring at the tea getting cold.

"Having dead relatives is, too," I say. "So, where's the rest of your money?"

"I had to reinvest it into the company—"

"I'm not going to chew on that shit anymore like it was some goddamned bougie meal. I swear I'm going to make your girlfriend throw up whatever money you fed her. Or shit it out. One way or another, I'm getting that money out of her."

"You're so crass."

"And you're a brother. Act like one."

"Fine, geez, I'll figure something out."

Visiting the Dead: A Memory

In the early hours of morning before we go visit the dead, the cock crows. The air is dusty with night and moonlight. Footsteps tread through our home's long passageway to my bedroom. The door creaks open, and my body senses the intruder with anxiety. I'm sleeping, but my body is coiled with fear. Through the sight of my skin, the intruder is bone-thin, moonlight-soaked and wan. It is Grandma in dreamskin, lacking flesh and fat. There is no shadow to her form. Her legs are brittle, her white gown embosses her skeleton in feather-form and light. The moon's lazy eye follows her footpath.

Dreamskin Grandma stares at me until I wake up from the intensity of her observance. My eyelids pull back, my heart bangs against my chest, and I'm quick with sweat. Dreamskin Grandma neatly and quietly wraps her bone-fingers around my throat, telling the air to back out from my lungs. She presses me hard that I can't move but to stare with nauseating fear.

"You're in the wrong room," I stutter. "Grandma's in the other room. You have the wrong person. You're warning the wrong person." I don't say I don't want to die but saying that means I want my grandmother to die. "What do you want?" I cry.

The dark sockets of her skull gleam with a thick torpid smoke. She speaks without voice: *Your genes are concentrated with a nightmare.*

"I don't understand," I say.

Little girl do you understand how difficult it is to mine dreamskin and extract from them a bountiful resource? Here you are mimicking me to a threat instead of seeking me as power. There are enemies who alter your vision so they have power over you. To have vision is empowerment—freedom.

"But I don't want to die."

Even if I were here to kill you, it would be the fake you that dies...not the real you.

"The fake me?" I look about me, unable to find an ally for escape. "What's so fake about me?"

The fake you is not this color, is not this hair. You questioned it before. If you are like the citizens from The City on the Other Side, then why is there a dividing line between you and them? Why do they receive more benefits? You are unconscious to the spiritual submissiveness that tethers you to the religious web of this city, thinking it holy. The fake you is a manufactured avatar by this city's ideals. You are a pawn in the grand scheme of things. Your sight, your hearing, the gem dissolved in your skin, the language on your tongue is a product that neither profits you nor promotes you in this 'beloved' city. You think you are invisible, that is nothing! Wait until you are not white-washed but turned translucent. Do you want to see?

"See what?"

The truth. Feel the truth. Bleed the truth. The world you so blithely desire is already here in your mind, penned in by their *laws*—she points in the direction of the other half of the city—*Break the walls and you are free.*

I'm thick with sleep and terror, a dizzying concoction.

"You're speaking philosophies and metaphors—you've lost me," I say.

Your great-great grandfather gave you sight, the dreamskin mimes, grime on its bones. *I will give you auditory gifts more valuable than the market value of your family estate.*

In the dark, my tongue traces my lips with hunger. "What must I sacrifice?"

Let me touch you. I will be your alchemist, not death.

Dreamskin. They curse, they destroy, they do harm. I will not be seduced by a dreamskin. "I'm fine, thank you, but Grandma's bedroom is down the hall, third door on your left."

Its form heaves forward, a menace steaming in its sockets like empty graves waiting for corpses.

My heart is a tolling bell. "But I said no," I shout.

Its cackle sparks the night air, and I feel stupid. *Child, I am not your subordinate for you to assume that you have the power to say no. No? To a dreamskin? Unheard of. A calling is an irreversible chemical reaction. I am here to dispatch what I must dispatch...into your body. Whatever dispute you have is not under my jurisdiction. See, I am quick to catch my death, it's a punctual train; I must not be late.*

The fucking dreamskin has humor.

"Nice pun," I say, bitterly.

Its claw snicks my forehead. *Politeness is my policy; I motioned 'choice' to you, not that you actually had a choice. You held the assumption of power.*

"But why?"

Trust no man without a shadow, it repeats a mantra. *If shadows are felled from their owners it means the body is vacant of a spirit. Something felled them.*

I never understood that statement even when Grandma repeated it. "Everyone has shadows," I say.

What the eye doesn't see, it assumes, it explains. *Conforming, you will lose everything that is dear to you. Time! Now lay still, I despise fussy prey.*

What am I not seeing that I'm assuming? Too late.

Grandma in dreamskin lays around my skin, an itch of a nightmare. Her bone-fingers remain imprinted to my neck. I try to scream for Brother, but her hand nullifies my voice, squishes it between her fingers like crumbled balls of sugar. "You're committing perjury," I try to scream. "You can't do this. Why are you doing this to me? What are you doing?"

Without voice, she maintains: *We make the rules, the rules do not make us.*

Fear explodes in my body; I pray to God. I stay paralyzed hour-upon-hour watching her knitting dread into my being: she raises her arms, a pantomime, drags them across my limbs, massaging something cold and soulless into me. Time sweeps out from my bedroom like dust in the hand of a wind until the walls are lit with the morning sun. Morning. My eyes see reality bare of a dreamskin figure. My bones crack as I sit up. Grandma's dreamskin visited me instead of her. I must break the news to Grandma of her death to come.

Brother slides open my bedroom door finding me wet with sweat. "Grandmother went to sleep and won't wake up." He is curt, unsure what to do with his body. He shuffles to and fro, shaking sweat, worry and uncertainty from his wrinkled forehead. "I can't hear her heartbeat."

Sister-In-Law appears and folds her arms. "She's—"

"I don't understand," he says, glaring at her. "No one dies without their dreamskin signing the death register." He holds up the leather-bound death logbook that holds countless of our lineage's death signatures, and next to Grandma's name is an empty space. I don't tell him that Grandma's dreamskin was too busy terrorizing me through the night to sign anything. I feel embarrassed and ashamed, but I don't know why. A dreamskin is only allowed one visitation in its entire lifetime: to warn the owner of their death to come. It is bad for it touch someone who's not its owner; am I bewitched? In the coming days, what symptoms will I display? No, I must not tell them.

"She's not dead." Brother is stern. "She's not dead until her dreamskin informs us. I refuse to believe it. We are not burying her."

A quick, cold fear blazes in my legs, halting the feeling in them. "If we don't bury her, we are desecrating our family rituals," I say, getting off my bed onto shaky legs. "Our actions will burden us with a curse."

"She. Is. Not. Dead. Not until her dreamskin tells us." He lifts the thick-padded logbook again, as if it's more alive than Grandma. He shakes it with the desperate certainty that the empty unsigned space is more definitive of her aliveness than the explicit death in her wordless heart. "It is not signed, which means she wasn't warned of her death. She can't die without being warned."

"They make the rules, the rules don't make them," I reiterate in a whisper, understanding what that future-ghost, the death-warner, the dreamskin said last night; they are not bound by the law to warn their owners—they can change the rules as they wish. But why, of all the four people—Brother, Sister-In-Law, Niece, Grandma—living in this house, did it choose me?

Brother narrows his eyes. "What?"

That I had a chit-chat with a dreamskin is not a casual thing to mention. They are feared and only revered for their prophecies, the ability to foretell our death for preparation's sake. But what if it was tricking me last night?

"What?" Brother enunciates.

"We have to bury her," I say.

"Dreamskin aren't allowed to do this!" He spits as he shouts. "This is the second time they've done this to *my* family. Unbelievable. I have to file a complaint."

"*Your* family?" My nerves twist in irreparable anger. "Listen here, I am not your property. You are not my commander. *You* do not make the rules just because you have two sacs hanging from your manhood. This is a family discussion, and it stands that we will *always* follow the rituals." Deaths in the family always birth warring parties.

"I am the head of this family!" he yells. He knows it burns me with anger, because yelling is kin to talking down to someone.

"*You* are not God." I, too, stand taller, and I pierce him with my glare. "It may suit you well that you delay with the family's payments, but I will not let you interfere with grandma's journey to the ancestral realm. Say that you are the ruler of this family, and I will sharpen your words and guillotine that 'head'" I step toward him, a heavy hold in my glare. "You want to take *death* and the dreamskin to court? That doesn't exist. Dreamskin are nightmares that don't always come through the night. Brother, these things are beyond us. Don't wrap Grandma's body in a coffin of legal shit. It's not as like if you win a case, then she'll be alive. We have to send her well according to the ancestor's dictatorship."

Brother shakes his head and storms down our passageway, patriarchy thick and intoxicating on the tongue of his mind. Bastard has too much pride to shed a tear.

Sister-In-Law comes towards me, snaps a strand of coiled Afro from my scalp.

I smack her hand. "Ish, man!"

She observes the strand in the sharp sunlight. "Your

hair is grey with death. Her passing has stained our house. We'll have to shave every hair on our body to be pure again."

★★★

Hours later in our hairless bodies, Brother is hasty with the ticking time given by my uproar earlier. He's delayed Grandma's spirit, imprisoning it in cold flesh for his stubbornness. Grandma's swollen eyes stare at the ceiling; her spirit scrapes the words "Hurry up, I want to die, to leave this imprisoning body" across her vocal chords. Brother brings an inyanga to the house, who declares Grandma's death and signs the death register on behalf of the dreamskin. The inyanga stares at me; her skin expands at the pores and sniffs the air, my essence. Perhaps it's the stench of the witch *crafted* into my skin that makes her sneeze and cough. She seems to want to say something but thinks better of it. Instead, she pats my shoulder and whispers secretly, "My condolences," as if I'm the one who's lost my life. Her voice is wet with cough. "Live, dear child, live. For that is all you have. No flesh is more powerful than God nor more powerful than your ancestors to take that away. Live."

I take her words as holy and anoint my hope with them. Do I dare pull her back and ask her what happens to those burned by the hand of a dreamskin? Do I dare risk my freedom, to be thrown away into a life of a pariah to waste away in the forest? Or worse, if anyone finds out, I could be killed and sold piece by piece and used as muti to pepper peoples' desires with juju. They will consider my body, incensed by the dreamskin's touch, more valuable than an elephant's tusk or a diamond. No one must know. No one must see. I shut my lips and move forward with the rituals of the day.

We prepare Grandma's body, wash it, and shave off

her hair to ease her journey. We bury her in the graveyard behind our residence, and scatter sorghum grains across it so our fields will be rich. We pour water over it so she can satiate herself on her journey. We wash ourselves of the death that has smoke-clung to our skins for several days without leaving our houses in fear of polluting our neighbors. Hours later, as the sun soaks the sky with its first light, Brother and I are at the train station with empty stomachs and fear saturating our bellies.

"Do you think she'll make it in time?" he asks, huffing into his hands. A puff of vapor escapes, rises like a cloud of smoke and disappears. It is too cold even for Grandma's spirit to journey into the train. If she doesn't make it, she'll remain trapped in our dimension as a silly ghost, growing dumb by the minute.

"I wish we could help her," I say, shaking on the spot, hoping to create a bubble of warmth around me. My bones are painful against my thin, tawny skin.

At eight, the train's horn signals its arrival, which is meant to wake her spirit up. Brother's head perks up. I yank my woolen hat down my ears, my teeth jittering.

"The train's about here. She hasn't risen from the grave yet!" he shouts.

How did it happen? You keep asking. It's been hours since we buried Grandma. You asked me once how Grandma passed away. I don't like talking about it because before she died, her dead-form in dreamskin visited me instead of her. I couldn't even break the news to her in the early morning of her death to come. Before the burial, her body looked thin and taut with death. It didn't look like her.

The train's wheels wail against the track as the train rattles to a stop across the platform from us. The conductor eyes us and Brother approaches him with ease and agility to persuade him. Finally, we see Grandma's spirit creep through the thicket of trees in the graveyard with shaky, weak knees, covered in cowskin, making her way towards the train stationed by the platforms. She is embossed in feathery light. The land is steep towards the train station, and she holds onto loose grass that crumbles down with fresh earth. My heart is in my throat, because I always helped her walk. What if she comes tumbling down and fails to board the train? It's happened to those who died in our wards. Their spirits wander the streets, listless, like torn bags of plastic. Time kneads them into bitterness, and they're no longer as kindhearted as they used to be. You find them in the streets, barking sometimes, chasing away the street dogs. Brother hugs me as we watch Grandma pat her weak knees and resume her walk on levelled ground. Her tiny hand is steadfast, holding a Bible.

When she steps into the train, punctual as usual, for the departure time, our hearts become lighter. Maneuvering to her seat, she opens her Bible and begins reading. We remind her to greet our dead great grandparents and parents for us. Our hands are still cold and high in the air, waving her a safe journey as the train remains still, waiting for its departure. Through the tiny aisle, dead Grandpa hurries to her with weak knees and stumbles into her lap, hugging her in tears. He can't hear my yelp of joy of seeing him.

"I really wish I could see where the train goes," Brother says, craning his neck to get a better look at Grandpa.

The city boundaries end in abyss-dust and black fog. The train disappears and remains there during its weeks of inactivity until it must come back out for the dead we have buried. I don't know what those like my grandmother do on that side. The train for the dead passes every once a month, and those who have died have to wait for it.

Today, like every month, everyone we know is gathered on the platform, our heads covered in cloth, hoping we get to wave or see our other dead relatives smiling at us. The train arrives at eight a.m. and leaves within 15 minutes. It is important that every citizen of the wards visits their dead relative. The relationship with the dead must never be severed. Dishonoring visitation rites will shame the family and bring misfortune to their lineage. When we visit Grandpa, he normally asks how we're doing and nags my brother to marry his girlfriend. He spends most of the time playing with Brother's baby. But right now he's too preoccupied with Grandma, his still-wife who's no longer widowed. Sister-In-Law can't visit because she must first be introduced into the family through marriage. At this thought, I catch Boyfriend smiling at me through one of the carriage's windows. Guilt makes it difficult to swallow. He thinks I still love him, especially after he died saving me from the fire of one of our outhouses. His face is knotted with burnt skin, scarred with my infidelity. I feel guiltiest when I kiss my Girlfriend knowing that he hopes we'll be united in death...someday.

Brother nudges me. "Don't just stand. Blow the guy a kiss or something."

I hesitate, raise my hand. Boyfriend's eyes brighten. On the cold fogged window, he writes with his finger: *I love you, s'thandwa same. I'll wait for you forever.*

Even when I die old and meet you as an old woman? I used to joke. But today the words are heavy anchors in my gut.

"Tsk, tsk." Brother shakes his head. "Shem skepsel. If only he knew you're cheating on him."

I elbow Brother in the ribs. "Shut up. The dead have hyper-sensitive hearing, you bastard." When I look back, Boyfriend is gone. Did he hear? Cheating on a ghost is really a new low for me.

Brother giggles, fighting me off, bumping into passers-by. We're not the only ones here. A couple of our neighbors stand eagerly to introduce their babies, wives, and husbands. When one of the carriage's doors open, a kid makes a lunge for them. The entire universe freezes, the span of a bird's wings pause mid-flight, the arc of air stills. The crowd of visitors cup their mouths shaped in terror. My heart leaps like a light ball into my throat, the blood in our veins stalled with panic. The kid's foot is literally an inch away from the riser, the father yanks the little boy by his corduroy straps and wraps himself around himself, fear pale on his face. "What did I tell you? You should never, *never ever,* enter the train. Never!" The young boy starts crying, and says, "I just wanted to surprise Mama."

If you enter the train of the dead whilst alive, you will never return.

Warmth returns to my cheeks, but I still feel the cold threat of dreamskin Grandma's bone-print grasped around my throat, a nightmare I may not escape.

You can't be near the dead without catching their fever.

The Mirror

We are nameless.

I can't remember them. I can't remember the people I loved. Where are their names? I wake up; we are burning. We have no names. I wake up screaming again. Every single time after seeing our passed-away relatives. No one hears me. My family chooses to not hear me anymore. Before, they used to think assailants were attacking me until they found an empty bedroom and a girl fighting the screams from her throat. I probably wake up like this because of what people say: our family is diseased. Even though we're all the same. I'm worse now.

Sister-In-Law and Brother never wanted marriage. They've had a bastard child. Our neighbors hate that fact; they have tall walls hoping that philosophy won't crawl into their homes like a thokolosi and possess their children. It happens often that the measure of protection is both preventive and useless. A few days ago, I found Neighbor 4201 in the streets on his knees, picking at a scrambling insect in the sand. He mindlessly threw it into his mouth and chewed relentlessly. Right next door is a unisex dormitory full of people fevered with the passion to not eat, which has the bodies of our neighbors constipated with pica, eating the shells of insects and crusts of plaster. Most people have their own beliefs which oftentimes noose our necks and deform us into strangers living in our bodies. So our neighbors keep sight of us and lay certain pieces of herbs around their yards to dissolve our fate from stealing into their homes.

The District on the Other Side of the City doesn't have horse-shaped wards like us. Their structures for living are ordered in grids as if in formation to a strict teacher with a lead ruler. When I wake up, the sun is a swollen eye in the sky, burning the morning into nothing. I wonder how The District on the Other Side of the City wakes up with no sun, no warmth. The rooster crows for the millionth time, its flapping wings like someone clapping, and I wish I could snooze it. It sits on the thick log outside my bedroom and if I stretched my hand out my window, I could strangle it. I try to beg sleep to not leave me, and it reconsiders, but the bustle of morning noise from my family members evaporates it: the baby crawling through the hallways making murmurs of nonsense, Sister-In-Law shouting "fotseke" at the street dogs that have somehow snuck into our courtyard for our garbage, a splash of liquid into the courtyard, my brother's shoes making a stiletto noise on the stone floors. I feel sorry for Sister-In-Law. Fotseke. At least we still have our language, this gem of a stone that I crave every second of the day, the way it bends and melds into the air, dissolving sweetness into my ears.

"Eish." I groan into my pillow. I can hear who I am. The real thing, she said, I would become the real thing. I want to tell everyone, share it with them, but that would reveal that I was touched by a dreamskin. But...this doesn't feel like a curse...unless it will slowly evolve to evil. Live *is evil spelled backwards. We are living evil*, my Girlfriend always motions. I rattle my head of these confusing thoughts.

I pull the blankets aside, and they smell of urine. I've

wet the bed again, like always, since I lost Grandpa. My
family, when they were still alive would ask me, "How
were you dreams tonight?"

"They were tough," I'd always say. "That's why I wet
my bed." My skin is a parched brown; I remember
screaming, after Dreamskin great-great Grandpa visited
me four years ago. My skin—what happened to my skin? I
kept shouting at the whole household, reckless with fear.
My skin wasn't like the cow's milk we drank every
morning, it was desert-sand brown, terrifyingly beautiful.
I'd never seen anything like it except of those on the train.
I *actually* thought I was dead for the only time I saw still-
Black skin was on our ancestors, cloaked around their
skeleton majestically, and now, I wore that coat. My family
couldn't see my skin the way I saw it. To them, it looked as
white as the mist that skidded the Badimo Mountains
flanking the entry into the abyss where the train embarks.
They did not have the sight.

This morning, my skin is different, as if the casual
terror from my dreams diluted it during my sleep. *What
was I dreaming of again?*

The bright morning light streaming into my window
sullies my sight, wringing a sick headache into my mind.
My knees are shaking. My Girlfriend is coming today, and I
don't want her to see me this way. She'll crack me open
and I don't want to wash her with my secrets. I do not
want to taint her.

"From foul dreams comes the stench of creatures of
evil," Dreamskin Grandma whispered that night, standing
over my bed, her eyes a cloudy cataract. That day she
looked like an apparition, the one that slipped from her
dreams to tell her that her death was close. Instead, it crept
into my room with wiry legs and held a cold grip around
my throat, leaving a soot-marked necklace of handprints.
The memory is unbidden but it comes for a reason, a

reason I do not want to know now. I lock the secret in my body. No one will ever know it. No one will ever see it.

My bedroom door swings open.

"Your brother's slaughtered the cow," Sister-In-Law says. "He wants us to make segwapa." Something about my appearance widens her eyes. "What were you dreaming just now?"

"I can't remember," I whisper.

She pulls out table salt from her apron's pocket and throws snatches of it over both shoulders. I roll my eyes.

"How will you know if anything bad will happen to you if you can't remember your dreams?" she asks.

My palms are pale and wet with sweat. I ignore her and try to stand—every bone is brittle and I hit the floor. Sister-In-Law tries to help me but shakes back from the urine smell. "Giiiirrrrl," she says, walking back, pinching her nose.

"Don't tell her," I say. "I'll be fine. Just don't tell my Girlfriend."

Sister-In-Law has an inch-layer of natural hair, which is decaying into sinewy strands. She is thick-set. Her skin is smooth and brown, the brown is melting from her. I blink and yank her arm towards me. The melanin is innocent and where it should be.

"What?" she asks.

I shake my head; droplets of sweat stain my night-gown.

She pulls back her arm, rubbing my fingerprints off her as if they are dirt marks. "I'll send you my quotation for the lies you want me to manufacture."

"Ja, whatever, man. Just don't tell her," I say.

"I wonder what else I can get from this amazing power you have given me," Sister-In-Law says.

I throw a pillow at her, she ducks it, but I can hear her cackling in the hallway. Jittery, I make my way to the metal tub. The daylight is still warm, so hopefully today I won't bathe in cold sunlight. Our bedrooms are spacious, allowing a workstation and a metal tub that stands in one corner surrounded by a gauzy curtain. The bamboo spout protruding from the wall oscillates up and down. I press it down and an oval opening in the roof shifts aside allowing a shower of sunlight to splay down with the passing slurp of time. I stand beneath it, washing away the sweat, the nightmares, and the memories. The sky is a quiet blue, a serene being massaging my body. As I'm bathing, I feel a rough patch on my lower back. It is a scab. When I peel it off to take a closer look at it, it's a plain piece of my skin color, not the hard covering of a healing wound. My bedroom door is not locked. A noise makes me quickly shove the patch of skin color onto the window sill where I encounter several more pieces I've tried to hide. Cockroaches scatter away from the pieces of my still-Black skin.

My skin color is peeling off. I am transitioning. Is that why Dreamskin Grandma visited me instead? What if the curse whitewashes me or worse turns me into a see-through? But what color am I? Am I really brown, or do I want to see brown? My dead family is still-Black, so that makes me still-Black, right?

The only thing I can trust to reveal to me what my back looks like is a mirror—something that won't make a fuss or discriminate me. In a desperate, senseless act, I dash to the useless mirror in my bedroom. Except the mirror does not reflect me. It shows a girl with ghost-skin. We don't have such mirrors in our wards: mirrors which we can use to recognize our true selves. Our mirrors only reflect those native to The District on the Other Side of the City—never us. No one in our wards is able to procure them. The only time we ever become us is when we're dead; when we're dead do we become the still-Black font of sky. I pick the thin pieces of my ethnicity, which are skin-thin, and raise them to the sunlight. "Cover me whole. Stay. Remain," I pray. "Stop leaving me. Don't leave me alone. Show yourself. Show *me*." I smudge the dead skin color onto my wrist, but it is brittle. It grinds like dead leaves into crumbs of nothing.

I slam my arm into the lying mirror. "Useless, stupid mirror," I shout. The mirror shatters. I am crazy, that's what Dreamskin Grandma did to me.

Sister-In-Law runs into my room. "What happened?"

Pieces of myself, reflections of me, stare back at me from the broken parts of the mirror.

They show a girl a shade that is not herself, eyes that are not her, hair that is not her. They show her a universe whose laws refuse her very existence. A girl who has never seen how she looks. A girl with eyes that can tell the original identity of people, except herself.

No one has these eyes.

My eyes became like this way before my Grand-mother in dream-skin strangled me. She was the second dreamskin in our family to strangle me after my great-great grandpa. I've lived this long, but why do they keep doing this to me? Why me? He gave me what the dead see: the sight of the dead. Now she's given me the hearing of the dead, for language, for dialect. Grandma said people like me don't live too long. There's a mirror that lies at the end of the rainbow that will show you how you look, say the fairytales. My Girlfriend would always sit between my thighs as I plaited yarn braid into her hair.

"Tell me how I look," she'd ask.

"You look beautiful," I'd say.

"No, tell me how I really look," she'd whine.

"You look beautiful. Your skin is the perfect measure of melanin."

"What is my name?" she asks. "What is your name?"

She looks around. "See? We are not important. We have no identity." She'd knot her fingers. "I feel that because no one can see who I am then I'm not real. I mean, if the people of The District on the Other Side of the City are reflected by our world, and it won't reflect us, that means we are meaningless."

I sat on my knees and pressed my hand to her chest. "There is air in your lungs. There is aliveness in your eyes. A law put it there. This universe wants you awake. You are real. *You* are my mirror. That is all we ever need of ourselves as a community. We are the reflections we want."

She yanked a chunk of Afro from her head, leaving a balding spot. "But this—what does this look like? I want to know who I am."

I curled my hand around hers. To her, her Afro didn't look like Afro. To her, it appeared bleached and strained of its length. To her, it didn't look the way I saw it: natural.

"Damn it! You think this shit is cheap?" Sister-In-Law shatters my memory, pointing at the broken mirror.

"I can't see myself," I shout, keeping my back away from her eyes. "I want to see myself."

"What's new? Damn it! I thought you were dying." She rolls her eyes. "Next time you break something, we're going to ignore you." The door shuts itself when she walks away.

Who will tell me how my back looks now? Soon I will have no more skin color—it's running out. What can I do to avoid replenishing it?

In our wards, people are lost to the evolving Loss of Sight or malevolent creatures. Prayers are so strong they can turn into creatures of evil. There are prayers of the bad kind. And our neighbors, jealous of the tenders my brother wins, are always praying. Maybe they prayed for this to happen to me.

The Loss of Sight has become a landmark, a postpubescent period that can happen to anyone in our wards. It terrorizes the body, but people still live with it lurking in their blood. Brother is sick with it. But he is still Brother. My Girlfriend won't—will never come near him. The fear is apparent in her eyes, even though she tries to hide it for me.

I stare at the metal tub shining under the sunlight and I need my Girlfriend to tell me I am okay, that everything will be okay. We used to bathe in it as it kept our bodies alive and warm. When the room was a mellowed gold, the silence a warm creature, she'd sit in the center as I poured sunlight down her head. Her Afro was thick and rich, and when I poured the sunlight through it, it made the same sound when the ocean pulls into and away from the shore, swelling and foaming. I closed my eyes, reveling in the memory, poured the sunlight again and listened to the sound of the ocean in her Afro. Thinking of My Girlfriend begins to thaw the nightmare's cold presence in my mind. If only I could murder these demons.

The District on the Other Side of the City

The city was divided in two by the train: on the east side, the sun rose and set; on the west side, the moon rose and set. Two different types of people lived on either half of it. No one crossed the railway line. One side venerated the other side. It doesn't take much guesswork to know which side that was: everyone wanted to see the moon, except me. It burned the dialect from our tongue, made us speak in broken accents, our mother tongue thick and deformed.

We live in the wards on the east side of the city. Our nights are always moonless for we have no moon. We are safer this side even though many prostrate it. They said the sun was the reason for the texture of our skin and so we bathed in it. The citizens of The District on the Other Side of the City have a different color of blood. The moon has an effect on them which makes them shed old blood and regenerate new blood. The moon tides their blood, it comes in waves into our land, packaged, and sells for high profits. They'd rather have our money then our lives. They believe that the train that divided our city in two is a myth, an unreal thing. It is invisible to them, except us. They never come to our wards because their blood has unfortunately become our totem, a totem we don't preserve but tear into. A totem of ours that is *preyed* on like a religion.

The people in our wards drink their blood like holy water hoping it will make them as beautiful as them. But the blood burns. Every three months, Mama—when she was still alive—used to sit me between her legs and oil my scalp with it. She'd say, "Sit still. Pain transmutes plainness into beauty." It felt like pain was peeling my scalp off my skull. Days would pass by and my hair would become limp and break off. The blood is a chemical that turns our hair straight and bleaches our skin. Our wards still love it either way. In the black market, it sells for high prices. The blood is processed, bottled, boxed, and sold by street vendors. My brother's girlfriend is addicted to this stuff, strutting around our residence wearing dead things on her skin and hair.

My brother's girlfriend, who I consider my sister-in-law even though they are not married, stomps into my bedroom. "Did you touch my stuff again?" she asks, holding an open jar filled with a colorless liquid: the blood of a citizen from The District on the Other Side of the City.

I point to my Afro, which I've seen for many years the night after Grandpa died, after his dreamskin visited. "Do I look like I touched your shit?"

Sister-In-Law narrows her eyes at me as if I'm a foggy shape. "Looks like your hair needs to *relax*."

That's what the stuff did. It apparently made our hair 'relax' because it was always held up in a halo, a science that The District on the Other Side of the City failed to understand because their hair always 'relaxed' down their shoulders and back, what became the commandment of beauty.

"Looks like alopecia is relaxing itself across your hairline," I say, working on my telescope.

She runs to the mirror, knocking her head against it, even though the mirror doesn't function in our wards. I wonder if the mirror showed me my true reflection, would it reflect to me the curse that Dreamskin Grandma imprinted on me?

"Mxm, that's not funny." She brushes down her baby hair with her fingers like a mime caught in the trance of its reflection. If only she could see the *real* me. Our senses— sight and hearing, but not the soul sense, for some of us anyway—are sedated, edited for our well-being. We've always known this since time immemorial. Every civilian in the city is a pale shadow of the moon, but the dead have always whispered to us what we are by the skin brown-stitched, taut to their skeleton. "Mama," I used to ask, pointing at my uncle, dead on the train. "Malome used to be moon-skin, now he has brown skin; he's your brother. If we're related, how come our skin doesn't look the same?" She pressed my lips down with chili and said death is an alchemist, transmutes the unspoken into its known elixir. We were elixir, she said, that reality couldn't translate. To keep us alive in the wards, this was how it "dubbed" us. But Grandma said, "Reality is some dictator's manufactured manifesto, but no one can evaporate the soul's dialect except us."

"You know what's not funny?" I say. "Cashing in on my brother."

"Your brother is a very accommodating person."

"Should my fist accommodate itself in your ass, then?"

She rolls her eyes and makes her way to the kitchen with me following her. "Did anyone ever tell you how crass you are? Like, are you too dumb to communicate in a more intelligent way?"

She places the jar on the counter and fetches a similar-looking compact bottle from the highest shelf in the kitchen. She leans her head back and presses it, releasing three droplets into each eye. She looks at me, blinking.

Her brown eyes have patterns of blue feeding into her iris, burning off the brown that made her softer. Her friend—with no medical background—prescribed her to take the blood three times a day until she felt satisfied with the results. And if she took it during Mass, or when the choir's notes reached a climax and the sun was in a froth of clouds, the marvelous effects would possess her body. At church, she'd wash it down with the Holy Communion or nibble on the blood curd during Mass. I wish she'd stop taking it; she has a beautiful voice, and it's slowly disappearing. She's been breastfeeding the blood to my niece and there's nothing I can do about it because she's the mother. There are days I wish for our residence to burn down with these jars filled with blood, but that won't stop her from purchasing more stock.

"I tried speaking to you *intelligently* weeks ago but you still didn't pay rent then. Maybe I should communicate with violence," I say, entering her personal space. I grab her jars. "These still sell well as second-hand products."

"Alright, chill. I'm plaiting three ladies today, I will give you the money."

She's knocked off-kilter by an invisible force and I the same, knocking against the kitchen shelves. Blood leaks down my forehead, a natural red color. For a second, I assume it's the result of the bone-print around my throat —I squeal in a hot torture of panic. What if my family gets attacked because of me? Some believe that once marked, an entity will slither beneath the strata, it will squirm beneath the house of one marked by a death-warner not meant for them. A tremor shakes our residence. Screams and shouts scrape every surface of the air. Doors bang, footsteps skid, furniture falls. Every time the train moves in-between our districts, our wards are the only lands to experience its effects snaking beneath the strata of earth that our buildings are rooted to. Cracks scatter our walls. Sister-In-Law runs for her crying baby and we flee through our entrance gates. Sirens sound, and our far-reaching residence leans to one side. It doesn't topple. We think it will collapse but it stays frozen in space. Everyone in the neighborhood is out in the streets, dismayed, shaking their heads, like one mass of anger.

"This is fucked up," says Neighbor 4302. "The city needs to update the architecture. It's going to bury us one day."

"They believe that we're the cause of our urban disorder," says Neighbor 4301.

"But it's the train that's causing these earthquakes," says Neighbor 4297.

"Earthquakes that The District on the Other Side of the City doesn't feel," says Neighbor 4305.

I fold into myself. Guilt is a flame on my skin. It is not my fault. I am not the cause of the disorder in our neighborhood. They earthquakes have been occurring way before I was touched by Dreamskin Grandma. But what if there are others in hiding, skins wrapping secrets?

Earthquakes only destroy the lives of those living in the wards. The citizens in the districts are immune to it. Sometimes I wonder if a god decided whom suffering clung to, for it was particular to us, not them. It must be nice to not be targeted by earthquakes, to be free and who you are.

"Just because they don't feel it, doesn't mean it's not real," says Neighbor 4302. "There's a reason the earthquakes are targeting us, that something rotten harbors. Evil doesn't just come from nowhere for nowhere. *Something* attracts it."

I feel his gaze on me, a heavy shadow. I shuffle closer to Sister-In-Law. But he continues to stare.

"You know why," he says.

I am naked. I am burning naked.

"Your brother," he says. "He develops the built environment. *You* must know something."

I sigh, releasing the weight from my lungs.

"They, the other side of the city, instigated them," says Neighbor 4295, spit spraying the congregation we've gathered. "They are doing this to us—they're abusing us!"

"We can't prove it," I regurgitate what my grand-mother fed me. "We don't know who built the train and the railway tracks and when it came into existence. Probably before any of us were born. Besides, each year most of the city's budgets are allocated to The District on the Other Side of the City."

"Have you seen the houses they live in?" says Neighbor 4302, lust dripping down his lips. "Towering buildings, taller than ours, that shine under the moonlight, and buildings with sky gardens. Their roads are a labyrinth of highways, they have buildings just to play in or relax in, they have—"

"Are you blind? They're so selfish they're eating into the sky now," says Neighbor 4303, staring at our earth structure towering into the jungle of sky and clouds. "One of these days, they're going to knock the moon down."

"The District on the Other Side of the City is running out of space," I say, recalling Brother's meetings. Brother runs a company that assists in new constructions, refurbishments and adapting old buildings to the city's fluctuating laws. He's handled the most lucrative tenders in our wards. But somehow debts slurp his profits, and we still manage to get by. "The city municipal is suggesting tearing down the railway line and restoring run-down nearby areas to accommodate the urban sprawl of The District on the Other Side of the City."

"Tearing down the railway line?" says Neighbor 4302; his eye twitches. He never believes what I say. "But—but that's where we bury our families—in the train. If there is no railway track there is no train."

Our families represent a culture we will never get back.

"Apparently it's taking up too much space," I say, and the words feel like acid in my mouth. It's so much harder to say than hear it from someone else.

"Our culture is taking up too much space?" Neighbor 4295 stutters. "But each district has the same meterage of land. We're all equal."

"We're *not* all equal," says my brother, who's appeared suddenly out of the corner of Neighbor 4302's boundary wall. He appears haggard and out of breath. His eyes rest on Sister-In-Law and their baby and relief paints his face handsome. His hair is ghost-color and wiry, tied into a tight puff that he runs his sweaty hand against. "Are you both okay? I rushed here the minute I felt the earthquake. The civic center came down. I thought something bad happened to you."

But everyone ignores his remarks.

"And who will be the labor force in these new constructions?" asks Neighbor 4302.

Brother stares at me and I expect him to admonish me later. "The labor force will come from our wards," Brother says. "It will create jobs. Both in the demolition of the railway and construction of new buildings. Demolition of the railway will resolve The District on the Other Side of the City's overcrowding, traffic congestions, urban sprawl—"

"What about the train?" I ask. He hates point-blank questions that are too heavy to handle in crowds.

"They see no reason for its existence because they don't see it," Brother says. "The only thing they see is railway tracks demarcated with a wall on their side. A burial site will be dedicated—"

"The train *is* our burial site," I say. "Our ancestors live in there. Are we supposed to hand them eviction letters and everything is hundreds?"

"They. Are. Not. Our. Ancestors," Brother enunciates. "They're just dead. We're not supposed to see our ancestors like that. Besides, the train is a transitory space for them. They don't actually live in it. Technically we're not kicking them out."

"They still mean something!" I shout. Neighbor 4302 nods in pride, in ownership of what I say.

"Soon you will be seeing some urban features to help facilitate the urban planning of the city's infrastructure," Brother says.

It's the way he pronounces the word 'urban features,' like he's shoving it under the carpet, dressing its true identity.

"What urban features?" I ask.

"Do not panic, every improvement made is for our convenience," he says, side-eyeing me.

"The fact that you tell us to not panic only raises our eyebrows. Why is 'panic' a thesis to your statement?" says our scholarly Neighbor 4302.

"Well, change is always scary, and the new presence in our streets will look quite conspicuous, and our *superstitious* fellow citizens are infamous for treating unknown things as, well, insidious. Which is not the case!"—he raises his palms truce-like— "Just remember it's here to watch for out safety." Vague is Brother's middle name.

"Watch for us or watch *over* us?" I ask.

Brother sighs, runs his hand across his face. "I trust no one will provoke our guardians, the new urban features. It's been a long day. I'm going to retire to bed."

"What will happen if we provoked them?" I ask.

He says, casually, "It's perjury. They will impose the law on you as they see fit. Right. On. The. Spot."

The neighbors shake their heads, murmuring, walking

away.

"The money," I say as Brother walks away relieved.

He spins around. "Shit."

"You forgot? Are you kidding me?"

"What about the tenants' money?" he asks.

On one side of our residence, we've rented out three rooms to three quiet widows who have shaved heads covered in headscarves. They pay their rent timely, but their walls have become pocked with their woes with time to leave their skin unmarked with wrinkles.

"Used it already," I say. "You can't tell me you forgot."

"I've had a hell of a day—"

"Your grandmother, your brother—"

"I know! Keep throwing it back in my face. Goddamnit!" He walks away. It's days like this I miss my sister. She was the only one who could work my brother. The door bangs and silence retreats into the cave of my mouth.

I am submerged in an ocean of things I can't control: a curse noosed around my throat will call on me, will cash in on the debt of life I breathe—how in what way I do not know but all the air in my lungs has to be enough to save my grandmother, my grandfather, my ex-boyfriend—my dead family before I become dead. The train will be destroyed, we'll lose our ancestors; we'll lose ourselves. Our lives will be erased. I stare upward, the sun bleeds into darkness, nighttime.

Nightmares, nightmares, wretched things.

A Love that Someone Lived Before Us

Conforming, you will lose everything that is dear to you, she'd said.

Another dreamskin visited me last night. It resembled my lover and I. It stood in an ocean of fire, foretold the end of our relationship and prescribed: "The church graveyard is a market store with rows of love, of couples who were buried together. Purchase their love to stay in love."

I am losing my sanity, I am losing my skin color—I will not lose my Girlfriend. In my storage, the liquid of love is running low. Only two droplets famish my tongue. I can taste the tears of my lover's sadness. We must go to the church grounds for our next supply.

My brother is in the kitchen laying out his work shirt on the kitchen island. The bulky iron is soot-marked, and it carries red-hot coals in its belly. Brother wraps his hand around the wooden handle and runs the hot iron over his shirt. The moisture in the shirt sizzles under the scalding heat.

"I know you worry yourself stiff about the family," Brother says. "I managed to borrow money from a loan shark and covered three months' worth of fees for our relatives. They won't be kicked out of the train. So go out and live a little. Take your girlfriend out." He laughs at the latter.

"I thought you were getting commissioned for these city projects," I say.

"There's a bit of delay in processing the funds," he says. "Besides, building this residence took every thebe we had. So take time with your art, you don't have to rush it to make a sale to take care of us."

I stare at the table and suddenly realize this weight removed from my back. Three months I won't have to worry about payments that have to be made, or cupboards empty of food.

"My girlfriend says you wet the bed again," Brother says, pressing the iron harder against his shirt.

"I haven't been able to see things clearly," I say, crinkling the skin-color that peeled off this morning

"How old are you again?" Brother asks. "Remember I lost my sight two years ago?"

We're not blind, we're only born blind to each other's true identity. The older we age, the worse it becomes, which is why we call it the Loss of Sight, a dementia toward the ethnicities we've lived in, bred under. It evolves to death or an opaque form of living—no one sees or hears you; oxygen culls your lungs.

"It happens sporadically that we haven't determined the age that people lose their sight," I say. "My time can't have come yet." I look up at him. "What will I forget?" I want to cling to myself.

"Your speech, your language, your skin, your hair." He stretches his arms wide. "All of this."

"The house?" I ask.

"Only how you see it."

"How do *you* see it?"

"It looks ordinary. Typical. Standard. Like a cubicle made of glass."

"Like a cubicle made of glass," I repeat. "Don't you

experience the emotions you evoked in this design?" He
shakes his head. It is a language I do not understand, does
that mean the function of the house is altered only to him?
Does it mean that the hallways do not exist to him as they
do to me? How do we exist next to each other yet exist in
two different realms within the hand of this very second?
Aren't our rooms organized the same way we experience
them? I know I pass the hallway and turn left to my
bedroom which overlooks a courtyard. Does he not turn
left, too, when he wishes to see me?

I bend my head into my thighs and weep for
something I am to lose. My brother does not wipe my
tears. He has been here too, and he has not died...yet. It is
nothing for me to cry over a pain someone has already
traversed.

"Does it hurt?" I push my words through the tears.

"It burns," he says. "Every day it burns. We've learned
to live with the pain."

"How do you live with it?"

"In life there is nothing to do except two things: live or
die. Being alive leaves you no choice but to survive."

"What do you mean it burns?"

"It's mystic. You don't feel it in your skin, it exists in a
plain somewhere within you. You go to sleep with the
burning sensation in your soul, you wake up with the
burning sensation; it is only within your dream are you
free. When we fall asleep, we enter our own universes
where we are free."

"So...you're burning right now?"

He sits the iron up, stares at the open cupboards filled
with herbs. "No smoke, no mirrors, no fire—but I am
burning."

"Don't you want it to stop?"

His irises are smeared with sky-blue, his body like my
canvass without paint without art. "No one wants to burn,

but unfortunately, it is us who burn."

"I don't want to burn...I won't allow it." My voice trembles. I stare at my fingers, the veins, the blood that courses through them with a naïve power.

His smile crooked, handsome. "Impossible is possible for the power of belief, the power of faith is a miracle enough."

"Then why don't you just believe?"

"It has been corroded by the ways of life, I lost it along the way and now I can't find it. You are pure—*you* still have it. You have Mama's strength, I see it in the logs of your ribcage, soul-lit, crackling, warm."

I sit my elbow on the dinner table under a sprinkle of sunshine and cricket chirps, my chin propped on my palm. "Remember when we'd sit outside in the boma, eating diphaphatha and Mama's morula drink? We'd sit and recite poems. I miss our family gatherings. Mama always made them special somehow." We both stare across the living room that filters out into the garden, and centered in the middle is the low seating of the boma made from the Badimo Mountains' rocks, trees gathered around us, bending their foliage-thick heads, leaning into our voice-licked stories. All three generations of our family would sit there, kids running around in the dark, playing silly games. The memory is sweet across the tongue of my mind, my mind salivates around it, sucks strongly on it, until the feeling turns to ember. Shadows and light crunching in the tall star-clustered fire. Soft earth beneath our feet, foot-prints and memories left in our backyard.

I will not burn, I will arrest my skin-color to my bones.

He narrows his eyes. "What boma?"

Empty space, empty bodies. The shadow by his feet retreats from the morning light, the sun cutting a line higher above sky.

I point to his feet. "Your shadow is afraid...of the light. It is shrinking."

"How is a shadow afraid of light that is its womb, its mother, birthing it? For a shadow to exist, light embalms it. Without light, there is no shadow."

"Without shadow, there is no spirit," I say, mind distant. "I don't want you to die, please."

"Are you prophetic now?" he asks. "I'm too busy to die."

"But your shadow..."

"My shadow is the one disobeying a law, not me. I'm here. Alive. Breathing."

"And your spirit...is it with breath?" My elbows, against wood, pain

"Your breath...is it with spirit?"

Paradox. I slouch in my chair, sulking. I'm never going to get an answer from him.

Cat meows, crossing in between my legs. It lunges onto the table and onto the window sill, watching something with peculiar concentration.

"We have a visitor at the door," Brother says, smiling.

My Girlfriend.

She and I started off as friends doing collaborations: she'd be the poetess, and I'd illustrate as she spoke; it was filled with drums, smoke, incantations, and the fumes of oil paint. We'd dance. We'd talk. As time crawled across the tense ligament between our unspoken feelings it grew taut until our tongues twisted against each other. Soon our bodies became the house of poetry. We'd lapse into each other, tangling into one fluid, cataclysmic art that relieved us into separate breathless bodies. She is the safe space for my secrets, and I the same.

She's always exploding with joy, it's contagious.

When I open our house door for her, she throws her body against me. I wrap my arms around her and she wraps her legs around me. There is no cure my body knows except this happiness. "Sorry, I'm late." She hops down. "I had the dream. Our dreamskins were trying to burn me."

"I'm sorry, love." The feeling is quick to attack me: my heart is empty. I can live without her. Signs that we need our medication soon.

"The sickness is getting worse," she explains. "I'm feeling empty, numb."

"We'll leave shortly. I'm still helping my sister-in-law."

"No probs, I'll just lounge in the courtyard." My Girlfriend kisses me as she tugs at my box braids. The pain hits me from nowhere: she doesn't feel me the same way I feel her—her natural self. A part of me I can't grasp is stolen from us. Would she love me if she saw me for who I am? When she touches me, what does she feel, what does she love? I tug back, thinking about the dreamskin tattooing me with a curse, a pain. My Girlfriend's lungs are balloons and I'm blowing in the hate and evil that my witch-crafted body can muster. What if I'm destroying her just by being next to her as our lips touch? I don't want my kisses to be her murderers. A piece of skin-color discretely wilts from my elbow to the floor, a brown flower petal. I'm falling apart. I shuffle my foot on top of it before My Girlfriend sees.

"What's wrong?" she asks.

I fake a smile. "I just missed you." She pinches my cheek and blows me a kiss.

A bold septum ring crosses her nose. Her long jangly earrings reflect the light as she walks. Her Afro is a halo that sits on her head, a place I love to get lost in. Her skin is an oasis for the sun's reflection, a warm brown that dazzles under its sight.

This is crazy, you only see this in The District on the Other Side of the City, is what the citizens of our wards said about us. It's supposedly why they named our house Ntlo ya Botsênwa: my brother with the illegitimate child, and my love as a woman with another woman.

My Girlfriend sits in the courtyard as Sister-In-Law and I are preparing the slaughtered cow's flesh into segwapa. A rondavel is on the far side where we've hung the strips of cow meat, waiting for it to become biltong.

"Those who've lost their sight are just that," My Girlfriend whispers, lying in the shaded verandah.

"Like what?" asks Sister-In-Law, and I want her to stop speaking, because her mouth has ruined kingdoms between people. If she tells My Girlfriend how sickly I looked this morning, it'd worry her. Anxiety doesn't flow well in My Girlfriend's body, and it'd break my heart if I put her through that.

My Girlfriend points to the strips of segwapa hanging on a line in the rondavel. Flies flit back and forth. "When I look around, I feel like we are like this segwapa, like we're strips of segwapa—dead," she says.

Sister-In-Law rolls her eyes. "Are you guys headed to the market?"

"There's tax to our love, my love," My Girlfriend says, looking at me. Her lips are painted indigo. Thick gold bangles encircle her tattooed wrists.

"There's a list of things we need to get for the house," Sister-In-Law says, ignoring her. "I placed it on the counter."

"Have you placed it with the money, too?" I ask.

She sighs, pulls slips of money from her bra. "You always think I'm out to cheat you."

"Because you always are," I say.

"And you don't even get taxed for loving her brother," My Girlfriend emphasizes. We weren't supposed to fall in love, so because "it stands outside nature and confuses the natural way of things" we have to pay for it before some god will repay "the debt through calamitous ways" and all that blah blah bullshit.

"Eish, I never forced you to love each other and pay exorbitant fees for it," Sister-In-Law says. "Damn, I walked into that one, didn't I? I wasn't trying to start a pity party. I just need things for the house. So please go feel sorry for yourselves somewhere else and don't forget to return with the house stuff."

My Girlfriend chews on an insult as she watches Sister-In-Law.

When I'm done helping Sister-In-Law, My Girlfriend and I make our way to the market, crossing streets, laughing and chatting.

"I hate going to the church grounds," she says. "I'm always afraid that we'll never make it out."

"No one but us can make the payments," I say, holding her hand.

"I know," she says. "It just creeps me out. Everyone there is so…unhealthy in their faith. They are so…"

"Passionate in the same way we are passionate about each other and our jobs."

She rolls her eyes and doesn't bother maintaining this conversation.

"Eish, there he is at it again, singing vile sermons," My Girlfriend says, looking at a beggar-like stranger walking up-and-down the street.

"Stop noticing him and let's cross quickly." I grip her arm and pull her hard. She giggles.

Beggarlike Stranger passed away last year and missed the train's departure time. So he spends his days on the streets, intoxicated and marinated in the heat of the sun, whistling at girls who pass by. The people in our wards ignore him. Sometimes he steals into houses and breaks windows. If you treat dead people like him who haven't made it onto the Train of the Dead as if they are human, like us, their touch is made real by our faith in their aliveness. And it's scary when people like him touch you. You feel the cold lick of death. It's bad luck. The only way to avoid him touching you is to pretend they don't exist; it's like a holy mark guarding us.

He limps toward us, grabs my Girlfriend. My reflexes are shadow-sharp; they betray me for they are quickly exposing the signs that I've been touched by dreamskin. I yank his elbow, steam hisses from the contact. He collapses back, palms outward, apologizing. Shock knots My Girlfriend's face, but she won't ask how I did that. It is reverse osmosis, reverse dreamskin. Their touch burns, now so does mine. My symptoms are ceaselessly becoming conspicuous, soon they will be a fully-fledged human being who will rat me out.

My thoughts itch: *I am sick with something.* I scratch myself until my nails dig blood. My Girlfriend and I make our way through the garden to an administration office that has become a lump to the side of the church of the wards.

I slow down, taking in the scenery on the way to the gates. The trees are large with heavy, bulbous fruits hanging from their arms. The garden smells of fresh earth and a rain to come. The sound of sunlight wafts across my face an intoxicating scent. My Girlfriend grips my hand and picks up her pace. "Don't even think about eating that fruit." That fruit got stuck in my father's throat. His throat is a huge lump. He sleeps in the tree, has become its bark, forever licking more fruits.

Approaching the administration office door, we find a young girl cross-legged with a mug of holy water. She is neatly tearing a Bible page, folding it into the size of a sweet and chewing it like bubblegum. She blows out verses that are specific to an infraction she committed. A Sister watches in the distance and whispers, "You will be good, child. You will be good."

"Parents send their children here to raise their school marks instead of sending them to tutors," My Girlfriend says, chewing on another inconceivable insult. "People come here for lost lovers, for marriage, for jobs without lifting a finger hoping for miracles to lubricate their lazy asses."

We hustle into the office. It has figurines made in wood and stone, and fragrances that call back memories we've never lived. The silence is moth-scented and wafts echoes of early morning prayers. The small office is heat-packed and stops the cold wind by the door's threshold so that it seems we exist in one season as we watch through the window another season force the trees into a manic dance.

My Girlfriend nudges me and points at stick-thin children playing outside in the church grounds. Their movements are measured into a slow pace. Pairs of children stand with a remarkable distance between them. Connecting the pairs is a line of wool tied to their legs, forming a fence for a queue of children to hop a pattern through, like hopscotch. One child hops in, hops out and rejoins the line. Everyone is quiet. Everyone is in sync. The game is so orderly for children, it traps me in its stately trance. I could watch them forever. The wind does not touch their hair plaited in symmetrical patterns of wool, the wind does not touch their skirts or the loose parts of their pants. Air is a viscous liquid around them. In the church grounds, no one relies on oxygen, on time, on human nourishment, only God.

My Girlfriend, an atheist, drags me to the counter. "This always happens to you. If I weren't here with you all the time you'd become a hermit in this place."

Coming here always brings the same nervousness I have for confessional.

A lady with dreadlocks is pushing snuff into her nose. She takes a cloth to wipe her mouth, sneezes and spits something out. She pulls a cane from its hiding spot and drags herself to the end of her office where she gives us an opaque bottle. "It belonged to a couple that departed," she whispers. "The love is intoxicating, but it cures every-thing." When she presses it into my hands, her arms are wrinkled with spots. "The only thing she eats is Bible verses. The only thing she shits are prayers," Sister-In-Law said which earned her a smack from Grandmother when she visited the house. I stare at the snuff the woman has hidden in her breasts.

The beverage is sometimes sweet, sometimes salty, sometimes tasteless. Its temperature fluctuates as its taste. It replenishes itself, not informing us of the day it will finish. The last one we bought only lasted a year. Without it, we became bitter. With it, we drink it with the idea of intoxication. Our actions to each other either demolish or preserve its longevity. The payments go towards main-taining the garden and the church's property. I jumped in the fire to stop our dream-skin selves from fading and found myself burning in love.

"Do you think it would be better to not drink this and be without feeling toward anything?" My Girlfriend asks. "We'd stop feeling sad about the to-be destruction of the railway tracks, of our homes, of the coming changes."

"We won't be sad, but we also won't be happy," I say. "I want to be happy."

"Ja, I guess you're right. You know, that's how they are. The Translucent ones." She stretches out her paper-white arm. "At first, we're like this, then we're...nothing. How come some die and some become Translucent?"

"Maybe it's a toss-up for the god of death. Angazi."

"I have a theory."

I smirk. "My sexy conspiracy theorist."

"The people from the wards are paper-white. It buries the ethnicities in our bloods. That's the first hierarchy of punishment. Second hierarchy of punishment is dedicated for people like us. We do not receive the privilege of death, we only become Translucent. I've studied the statistics. Remember my brother and brother-in-law?—they disappeared. Their bodies never turned up. Our city is surrounded by an abyss that no one can physically cross into. Both cities were searched, and not one molecule of their existence was seen. People like us are the only ones who disappear—they *literally* disappear *into* air. They're not dead, they're around us, we just can't see them."

Besides witnesses who've observed this disappearing phenomenon, how do we know about Translucents' existence even though we can't see them? The old lady who stays three houses from my house can see them. She lives with them. Has written scholarly material about them.

"...then those two lady couples were sighted at the park, and vanished into thin air. There were three witnesses..." she continues listing all the missing cases in our city.

I press my hand to her shoulder. "Then what triggers their disappearance?"

She stops, sits by the concrete seat in the garden where my father's skin marks the bark. "I don't know. That's what scares me. There's no telling! We could vanish now." She looks down at her bottle. "What if this drink is the cause of it? I mean all we know is it's the love manufactured from dead lovers, but what if the manufacturers add something else—it's not organic after all?" She looks up, blue eyes shining with tears, the image fizzles until I see her brown eyes with my dreamskin sight. "But if I don't drink this, I will stop loving you. It won't be painful because I will be without feeling. I won't feel anything but

I feel everything now, so I'm afraid to not feel anything then. I suffer the pain now."

This is a knotted complication. Can my dreamskin skills remedy this situation?

She cries into her hands. "I just don't know what to trust anymore."

I wrap my arm around her shoulder. "Let's not drink it."

"But I love you. I want to stay in love with you forever! It's not fair. The other couples aren't constrained to such rules. What higher power is giving others privilege?" Her body trembles and I rub circles into it.

"Listen to me. We are powerful. *You* are powerful." I raise her chin, wipe the tears from her face. "I will not allow someone's words to curate our demise. I believe in my existence. I believe in you, loving you. Your breath, your thought, your faith has unbelievable power, it curates miracles that will immortalize anything you desire. Do you hear me?"

She sniffs, nodding. "Where do you get all this faith?"

"Very simple. If you don't believe in yourself, someone's belief will kill you."

A quiet beat stifles the air. Her eyes widen, mouth opens into a silent O. "You're really special. I'm so glad we met. We believe so much in this drink that it became our truth, our reality."

"We will *not* disappear."

"But don't you think the others too believed in themselves? Why would we be the exception?"

The wind teases the branch above us, dropping leaves. One falls into my hand, and I fold it and fold it. "What if they wanted it? What if being Translucent isn't such a bad thing? People say dreamskin are evil, but they only open the door to a universe that gives sight. What if we're being fed lies about things that are good for us?"

"Why would you say that? Dreamskin are scary, monstrous things. I wouldn't want to bump into one at night."

I can't tell her. She'll freak out. Besides, I don't want her to get tangled into my mess.

"And why would being invisible be a good thing?" she continues, pressing her fingers into the concrete seat.

"What if you are being birthed into a universe, a dimension better than ours—that *we* can't see? And because we don't understand it, we believe it's insidious," I say.

She laughs. "And you call me a conspiracy theorist." Her eyelashes are lit with crystals of tears. I pick one and kiss her cheeks.

"I really do love you, you know. With or without the drink."

"But can we just drink it to be on the safer side?"

Her lack of faith pains me, but I smile for her. Anything to make her happy.

"We haven't yet lost our sight. Anything can change."

"It doesn't have to," I say.

"It's not something you can control." She looks at the trees in the veld. "My sister was set to get married. Lobola was paid and ceremonies were organized. By tradition they were married. When it was time for kgoroso, she lost her sight. I remember that morning, I woke up from my period pains, and I was going to use the bathroom. I saw her sitting in the metal tub in a pool of water. I was blind from sleep, and approached her with no cautious feeling in my bones." She closes her eyes and slips underwater. Anguish turns her body rapid. She comes up for breath and says, "The water was brown; she was Translucent. She lost her sight."

She pinches my skin with the intention to pull it apart. "This does not belong to us. If it belonged to us, it would stay. We are people with no skin."

"Stop, you're hurting me."

Shame pushes her back. "I'm sorry."

"You're being silly," I say. "Not everyone loses their sight. There's nothing to be ashamed of," I say. "My brother lost his sight—he lost his skin color, but he's still living with us."

"His eyes scare me," she says. "It's a cloudy blue, like a cloudy sky—it hides things. You're never quite sure what to expect."

"My brother loves us."

"Are you sure about that?" she asks.

"Why are you doing this to me?"

"I'm sorry," she whispers. "I haven't been myself lately. I get these thoughts a lot and they won't let me go."

"I'm here for you," I say.

"I know," she whispers, leaning her head into my shoulder. We lull in the safe waters of our universe until time calls us to reality.

"S'thandwa sam', ke a go rata," she says. "Soon those words will get torn down from our tongues and we will no longer be able to say them."

"I love you, too." I brush my tongue against her lips. "I miss your poetry."

"You're disappearing," she says. "I can feel you disappearing from my grasp."

"But I'm right here."

"Don't you know that you lose sight in other places before you lose it in your eyes?" she asks. "Say it."

"Say what?"

"Ke a go rata."

"I love you," I say.

"You can't speak it in our language."

"But I'm saying it: Ke a go love you." My teeth snatch my lips and the words become a rough stone. "I'm still here, please believe me."

"I will believe you only for you." She's always been stubborn in her beliefs.

"Let's go rest. I'm feeling sleepy," I say, anxious.

What if I'm disappearing before I've known it? No. I still feel the same way. I am me. She starts kissing every part of me, my neck, my breasts, my tummy. But there's an unusual religious fervor to her actions. "What are you doing?" I ask.

"I want your skin to stay, I want it to stay with me," she says. "I want to remember its taste."

That day, I remember what can't be erased, the traces her kisses left in my uterus, in my womb.

The shebeen was where people like us drank it in large quantities until it consumed them.

We sip on it on the way, a love that someone lived before us. I remember watching you bite your lip knowing that our waning love couldn't last despite how we tried bottling it for days we were angry.

My Girlfriend and I bunk work that day, staying in the fields, and drink until the dark buries the sun. We can't see much, so we take our bodies as light and sleep in its haven. What she breathes out, I breathe it in, and keep it inside me for the moments we are apart, something to feed on in her absence. I imagine our lives this way, growing old and happy. Being us. Forming happy with our hearts. The truth is dressed as a lie. They lied. It's been so good so far being touched by a dreamskin—how could it really get worse? I don't want this to change, being able to see her in full color and glory is not a curse; I'm glad the dreamskin touched me. All I need to do is keep quiet about this gift, and all this and eternity will be my life. My Girlfriend and I, we'll make our own estate, grow our artistry business. We are in command of our lives, and perfection is within reach—I really do feel it and believe the possibility of our dreams as vast as the universe, happiness shining within my chest. Nothing and no one can destroy the pureness of this feeling. It breeds eternity for us. It is not evil I pour into her lungs, it is the real us. "Ke a go rata s'thandwa same," I croon the silent song, against her lips, against her breath.

In the bleak of the dawn hour, a puff of cloud-dust explodes into the clear sky, the sound of thunder rupturing the earth. The ground quivers. Far out into the distant horizon, a giant knife prickles through the skyline of adobe settlements. A big bang in our soul-universe. We stare at each other, silence a blade scraping our faces apart.

It's not the train.

Demolitions have begun. The New Architecture dawns.

Cold, Uncaring Beast

"Is that a *huge* knife to the sky?" My Girlfriend asks, standing on a rock near the market place, craning her neck. "What is that?"

We're myriads of streets away from my home, but apart from the low-lying residences and estates, and adobe structures packed neat into the sky kingdom, from the huddled communion of our architecture, the triangular form pierces through the air, the clouds; bloodshed gleams across its steely skin, the sunset wails. The Triad, so says the sign blanketed across its façade, a chilling smile.

"Underground workers are fast," says Passer-by 1.

"Is that *the* resort?" Passer-by 5 motions.

"Ja, it will house residential units, recreational facilities, offices," says Stranger 1, shiny and raw like teeth. "Nothing like you've seen before."

"What about the neighborhoods that were in its place before?" I ask.

"Every tenant in that land sold their property. Relocated. We offered them more than the market value," says Stranger 2. He points at the new structure.

Ward 12 has just been taken down, quickly replaced by a foreign surgical tool. How did we not know this?

"The civilians of Ward 12 signed a confidential agreement before relocating from the premises," Stranger 3 says as if reading my thoughts. "Our firm uses a newly advanced technology that allows for quick deletions of structures and building constructions. It cuts down a lot of labor costs." The agreement was to create employment for our wards, so if they fell back on their word, what more will they refuse? A whistle parts Stranger 3's lips. "Now that is a quality standard of living. Which ward do you live in?"

I step back. His breath, his words are invading my personal space. "Why?"

"You might like it up there. There are units on offer. Here." Stranger 3 offers me a pamphlet advertising a residential unit.

"We can't afford this," I shout. "And they're so small— no garden space. We are comfortable where we're staying."

"They have a high market value. You'll love the view," adds Stranger 2.

"It'd be so much easier if we understood their language, quite irritating actually," says Stranger 3. "Well, it's something that can be easily remedied. Modified."

The ground beneath him is starved of shadow. I look up and back away. My Girlfriend notices it too, and beneath our feet our shadows war and flicker with something. I gasp. The District on the *Other* Side of the City! They are the Strangers, the Others; to not see their hand, we must not see their shadows' tracks. The Strangers with the Invisible Shadows.

"Hold on, how did you get in here?" asks My Girlfriend. "You're from the District on the Other Side of the City." Their skin looks like us, pale, ours mutated to theirs; there's a difference that discerns our side from theirs, a need be it seems.

"We're the architects, the proud brain power behind

this design." The three Strangers stretch smiles across their faces.

"But each side is not allowed to cross over to the other side," My Girlfriend says.

"Permission was granted given the new changes. Change is good." Stranger 3 smiles again. "I'm sorry— what's your name again, sweetheart?"

My Girlfriend zones out like her brain has ceased to function, a huge black hole in it.

"This place will be perfect for basking. It's beautiful!" says Stranger 1, admiring our region with bright eyes, staring in awe at the sunset. "And please stop referring to me as Stranger 1. My name is—"

My Girlfriend yanks my arm and drags me away, sullen at the lips. "They have everything, even names. What do we have? What are we left with?"

We're making our way home with bags rustling in our hands containing ingredients to help Sister-In-Law with supper. My Girlfriend asks me if what my brother reports in the headlines are true. I tell her I'm not sure, he's just trying to make money so we can survive. Our tongues have the syrupy taste of love that we don't notice a new urban furniture that stands in front of every residence in our neighborhood until we bump into it, falling onto our backs. Tall obsidian sentries with sharp angles, like a sculpture, cold hard forms, a dark hooded cloth covers them entirely.

"The Triad's sentries," says Neighbor 4302. "To watch for cases of crime breakout." The forms have no slit for eyes or mouth. We can't see if it has a body inside that cloth. Where the heavy fabric meets the ground, there is no sign of feet. Several of our neighbors are outside scratching their heads and waving their hands in anger at each figure that stands outside their residence's entrance. It stands in our path, a maddening smoke evaporating from its cloth. My Girlfriend and I try to circumvent it, but the boundary wall is protected by a myriad of them.

"They're Keepers of the Gate. They're security from The District on the Other Side of the City," says Neighbor 4302. "The authority assented to their existence and said we couldn't enter without its approval."

"Security for what?" I ask.

"Surveying for the construction slated this season. Our ward is the next chosen site," says Neighbor 4301.

"But this is our home," I say.

"The Strangers visited me today. They're offering good money," says Neighbor 4305.

"Did they give you a tour of The Triad's units?" another neighbor asks, excitement tickling his jaw.

Neighbor 4305 scratches his head. "I'm on a waiting list, so my family is renting out in another ward. The money was too good to pass by."

Something thick forms in my throat. Tears collect in my eyes. I will not let them fall. My Girlfriend fits her hand into mine, kisses it.

"But. This. Is. Our. Home," I whisper with a trembling voice.

Neighbor 4302 shakes his head. "Not today, kid. Try again tomorrow." He walks alone, he himself as his own luggage. The street looks so dusty around him that I want to hug him so the pain will leave our neighborhood.

My Girlfriend and I explain ourselves to the Keeper of the Gate, but as soon as we open our mouths to let our language flow from our throats, our throats become arid, and the air crackles with the dying beat of our dialect. A force stands in our vocal chords, a thick lump that denies both our speech, inhales and exhales. We don't know what language it speaks so we can negotiate with it. Even as we hold keys to our homes, the figure won't let us through.

My Girlfriend starts weeping and begins to drag me

away from the Keeper of the Gate. "Please, love, let's go before we get hurt."

Our distance ensures our ability to breathe. She's dragging me. I'm screaming. "The only thing we had left was our language. The only thing!" I shout. I want every creature to hear me, creatures that live beyond the sky.

The Keeper of the Gate has the power to null the language on my tongue. I try to scream for Sister-In-Law to open for us, but my voice can't climb over the walls, over the towers. It can't even reach the birds in the skies.

I scream and nothing scatters. Nothing can hear me. This is annihilation. This is murder. In their hands, Death is ceaseless; it is a cold, uncaring beast.

The Woke Rote My Bones Home

This place we call home took my skin-color, took my voice, took our hair.

Hours pass.

Days pass.

Weeks pass.

We wait.

We don't know if the Keeper of the Gate stands outside to protect us or to protect itself. But from what? But each time we exist in its presence, our chests become heavy with a paralytic pain and we slip into a vacuum, an abyss of silent pressure overwhelms our voices and the altars that hold our breath.

My Girlfriend doesn't want to go home. Home is an empty house. Her family is in the train. All of them—passage to the ancestral land. All of us *should* end up in the train; the train will be our home. But should we allow ourselves to be kicked out from our homes! My Girlfriend is a loner. Has always been a loner. The Keepers of the Gate scare her. We rent a hostel that night, and I hold her until her sobs turn into sleep.

I. Don't. Sleep.

I cannot sleep.

I am awake.

My anger is awake.

It is fed up.

It is saturated with woke that runs the valleys of our souls.

I am woke to everything.

It's the seventh night in a row I can't sleep and My Girlfriend wonders why sleep won't enter my body—*because it is not welcome in here*, I tell her—asks me what is wrong with my body and if the sangoma can prescribe something, or is it the syrupy love we've been wining on.

"When have you seen our love pick up a weapon and shoot down a man?" I say, throwing the beverage away. "What if the dreamskin people that prescribed this to us are manufactured by the citizens of the districts?"

"You need to sleep," My Girlfriend repeats.

I shake my head. "I will stay woke."

"You need to sleep," she says.

"It's too dangerous to sleep," I say. "I refuse to sleep. Sleep is a medicine they feed us to numb us. They're doing something when we're sleeping. Can't you feel it? Underground, beneath our feet, away from our sight, they're breeding their pleasures to destroy us. It shot out from the ground today."

She begs me to sleep, to think about my health.

I hold her and tell her, "The more I sleep the more I lose my skin—it's been peeling off for weeks."

She is stunned by this revelation. The absence of sleep allows the tales of truth to slip from my lips.

Tonight I am freedom. Nothing holds me back.

"You have to dream," My Girlfriend says. "In order to dream, you have to sleep. If you don't sleep, your dreams —your *nightmare* will roam with you unlimited by the hours of sleeping."

"Let them."

"They will hurt you. Please. Stop this insanity."

Within the sleeping hours, dreamskin people can wreck torture on our bodies.

I grip her shoulders. "Stay awake with me."

The hostel has only one bed shoved into a storage-sized room with a window to the sun.

My Girlfriend slips into the shadow of the sun. "I've heard of this 'woke'. It rots your bones. It leaves you out of comfort. There is no point to it."

"Lies. Lies. Like the dreamskin people they tell us about. They aren't monsters. Dreamskin make us alive."

She presses her palms to her ears. "Stop! No more. No more."

I step closer, eclipsing the shadow from her face. "What if this 'woke' will give you Sight? You will see yourself. You will see me. You will walk through walls. You will walk through anything." I touch my Afro. "This is a symbol I've been afraid to cut. But it is not me. This is me."

My Girlfriend catches me shaving part of my head bald. "What are you doing?"

"There is too much in me. I am going mad," I shout. There is catharsis in shaking your head loose of hair. Just because I have half an Afro doesn't make me any less deserving of its symbol. "I'm the girl with the half-shaved Afro." I stand tall, brandishing my shoulders. "I can see myself."

The ghost of a scream escapes her mouth as she faces the same mirror I'm looking into.

The mirror finally speaks truths. It speaks "me."

Boneless Shadow

The Shadow exists like air in our wards. There are days when streets or people disappear, or people we used to know aren't people we used to know. It's why we don't see ourselves in the mirrors. It's why earthquakes only occur in the wards. It is why the Keepers of the Gate have access to our homes. It's why our skins aren't still-Black font to stamp out words and preserve names. The Shadow's power wields through the streets in our wards to the veins in our bodies and does as it pleases. Its power is still at its low peak to conjure the worst damage. For now. At least The Shadow is not strong enough to destroy the train. We normally refer to The Shadow as They. It always feels like a group of people sucking the air from our lungs with their mouths and their straws for luxuries. But today, I am untouchable by The Shadow.

The melanin on my bones is a fabric quickly swallowing the sunlight. My Girlfriend is skeptical. She stares at me with lunacy rimmed around her eyes. She trails behind me, takes my kisses only to play nauseous later and vomit them out. She's afraid I'm leaving bombs in her mouth. I hold her hand to press the warmth of promises into it. "I am still the same," I say.

"You look the same, but you aren't the same," she

whispers.

"When you sleep, you look dead, my love."

She looks down, hurt.

"I love you," I say. "Trust me."

She wraps her arms around me; her scent is sunset-tinged. It leaves me breathless. Her tears rub solace into my back. "I love you, too," she says.

We stand in front of the Keeper of our Gate. It seems to have grown taller. I grip My Girlfriend's hand, and she squeezes her eyes shut as I walk passed the figure. It doesn't stir. I unlock the gates and we make our way to the front door.

I kiss her cheek. "Open your eyes," I say. "We just walked through a wall."

"We're home," she says, only it sounds like a question.

"We're home," I say. "Stay with me this time."

"What will the neighbors think?"

"They can go fuck themselves," I say, picking her onto my back and giving her a piggy-back ride into the house. Her mouth is no longer a desert of laughter. She is laughing and she is happy. That is my universe.

She hops off my back, her lips stretched down at the ends.

"What's wrong," I ask.

"Your house is different," she says. "It's been altered."

I don't see the differences but I walk her around and ask her to point out what's changed: it no longer bears the adobe brick for it apparently irritates the figure outside, it doesn't look expensive to it. She points at the new building material: the material shines, the material is cold, the material reflects. Only it doesn't reflect who we are. Sister-In-Law and Brother are not yet home to confirm what My Girlfriend says.

They call our house the house with the marigold windows. Its walls are mauve in some areas, and bright and muted in other areas. Our neighbors gossiped that our house wasn't built by science, it was painted. It turned shadows and light into beings that walk the passages and spaces. No one wanted it until they experienced it. Everyone now wanted the house with the marigold windows.

We built the house ourselves under Brother's apprenticeship within 400 sun days. The southern side was made in adobe, and the boundary wall of stone had a rusted plaque titled Ntlo 42301. The textured walls reflected the light so strongly, the pool of water did all to absorb and dissolve the light into itself, that in the common moonless night if you swam in it, orbs appeared in its body as if you were swimming in the buoyant nature of light.

I cross the courtyard, past the tree rooted in the ground with its brown skeleton deformed by lightning hands, leaving it naked of leaves. I knock on all the widows' doors. The widows welcome me back as I collect their rent. During the day, they chew seeds of a fruit, then plant it into each other's ears to prevent deafness.

The widows stay in their rooms and do not leave. Their heads are bulbous, smooth and shiny in the light. They know where their hair was buried, unlike ours that was burned. It has never grown back for them, ours is new and fresh on our heads. We don't know how long they have been mourning, but it seems like for years, as if they are sisters.

Our neighbors called them "dirty with death" for they are not cleansed of senyama—a toxic element to us and their new partners who will consume them. But we disregard it. They stayed alone because they still had senyama, it was not cleaned from them and the neighbors complained about it. They still slept on their abdomens without changing positions, they still ate goat liver mixed with herbs as if every day was the day their husbands died. People gossiped about them because their husbands weren't on the train or opaque spirits in the streets. Who were they mourning that we couldn't see? Did they hide their husbands' body or did they not send them off? Where do they come from? The day the widows arrived, knocking on our gate looking for a place to rent, the soles of their feet were soot-marked with abyss-dust. What mattered to us was that they paid on time. They do not disturb us, they do not eat much—all is well in our residence. Sometimes, when they stand in the courtyard, their headscarves are tied beneath their chins.

The night before, My Girlfriend and I listened to the tree tremble as the women ululated for the train's departure. They have already bought their tickets and are registered to board the train in two months once their lease has ended. Slowly, the rooms have become perfumed by the scent accumulating in their skin, a scent that calls scorpions to our courtyard into the outdoor fire which burns them into a feverish dance that crackles parts of them to the sun-marked sky. Smoke tangles in the mausoleum of the widows' lungs, their breaths a solace to those who visited.

In our house, geometric walls cut up the light into diagonal lines. The windows are tinted marigold to focus the majestic quality of sunlight so that it glows within the space, a solitary house that celebrates solitude.

"I feel something here," My Girlfriend whispers. "I sense something. There was an intention with the design of this house. The architecture does something to the light, it elevates it to its spiritual meaning. It moves me so much, it makes me want to strip and bathe in it."

I, too, couldn't understand why the light in the house was different, for it flooded the wards just as it did before, but it has been manipulated by the form of the building, by the glass in it, to appear mystic. It stirs something against my ribs.

At one end of the house, we have a room we called šawara, which is used by the whole family for cleansing. The pool water meets the wall and imitates a horizon, for the colors are placid and portray a distance that the horizon contains, the part when the sky is dilute. "It's a devotion to light, self, and the universe," I say. "It is pure from everything in the city."

"Can you swim in this as well?" My Girlfriend asks.

"Ja, it serves as a pool, too."

My Girlfriend's lips turn up at this. "Can I try it?" she asks. "Skinny dipping interests you much?"

We're buoyant in the sunlight-saturated pool. "Your house feels like a church," she whispers and her voice echoes. The square opening above us reveals a transitioning sky. The walls have texture. "I'm afraid," she whispers and turns away in embarrassment.

"What are you afraid of?" I ask, kissing her shoulder.

"That we will become different," she says. "That loving you won't feel like loving you anymore."

"That's jinxing us," I say.

Later, My Girlfriend is sitting in the living room by the fireplace, working through her mail, the baby crawling about her legs, trying to catch her bobbing feet. She has braids the thickness of my fingers that fall to her knees. Both are laughing. Sister-In-Law and I are preparing rabbit meat that Brother brought. She is mashing it into seswaa. We couple it with paleche, soup, and cabbage. During our meal, Brother tries to evade our questions about the city's new developments. Silence is the only thing that sits in comfort when Brother tells us that as long as we're related to him, we're safe. After our meal, I guide My Girlfriend to my bedroom. The hallway is cold. Our feet are bare. A shadow of someone passes our path into the hallway leading to Brother's bedroom. I crane my neck. The shadow has dissolved into air, and there is no body to claim ownership to it.

"What's wrong?" My Girlfriend asks, unable to pass through the barricade my arms have formed.

"I saw a shadow without a body," I say.

She cracks up laughing. "I had more to drink but you're way tipsier than I."

"It had no bones to hold it like us."

"You're shaking," she says. She tries to hold me together, but I am falling apart. I am a jumbled mess in the passage.

"I'm losing my mind," I cry. "I don't want to lose my mind."

"You're just drunk," she says, terror marking her eyes. "Please, get up."

I must get up. I must get up for her. "We need to evict them," I say.

"Who?"

"Them. Those widows. Those baloi people," I say. "They're witches."

"You're lucky you even have tenants," she says. "No one wanted to rent here."

"Isn't it better to be alive than have tenants?" I ask.

"Say something like that, and I won't return," she says.

"I know," I say, sadness pressing my face down. "I'm sorry. I didn't mean to scare you."

"You've made me sober now."

"We haven't run out of alcohol yet," I suggest.

A smile lights up her face. "Good idea."

I follow her, ignoring the shadow that appears again, walking back and forth in the hallway between Brother's bedroom and mine.

"Do you think I don't love you because I don't know how you look?" she asks when we settle in my bedroom, candles surrounding us in the dark that knows no moon.

"Where do you get that silly idea?" I ask.

She takes a sip of the liquid; it is as thick as blood. "I see the way you look at me. You look at me with loss, as if you're pleading with an imaginary god. I wake up with doubt, I go to sleep with doubt. You will leave me for someone who will see you as you are. Who will give you what you need."

"I don't know where you're collecting your fears from lately. Is there something you're trying to tell me?" I stand closer to her. "Wouldn't it be superficial if I just loved the skin on your bones? Have a little faith in your soul. I don't need its body to love you."

"You've given me a gift I can't give you: painting me, showing me who I am. This universe can't distort your art. It is truth. I feel like I shove lies into your body when I kiss you. Every day I wake up with this huge debt sitting on my chest—I have no talent to gift you with. Each day I'm trying to pay and pay but I keep failing. "

"You make me happy," I say. "You shouldn't need to pay, otherwise we'd both be broke."

She traces her fingers on my face. "I wish I had your eyes."

"I'm afraid envy will drown you, sometimes. I wish you wouldn't envy things you've never experienced."

She twists her lips, drinking again. "I know."

I pull the glass from her hand and smell it. "This is not the wine we brought with us. It is blood."

With casual occurrence, she takes it from me, drags another sip and says, "I know. *They* change everything whenever it suits them. They are forcing us to eat our people. To drink our people."

I throw the glass against the wall. It won't paint it red. The wall refuses our blood. It is The Shadow. It is Them.

"What is wrong with you?" I shout.

"I came into this world terrorized by the instrument

of death. I came into this world dead. My love, I am tired and I will accept what is." She kneels, runs her finger through the glass and the liquid, and sucks her fingers. "Whatever I eat is altered. Whatever my bones wear is altered. Whatever I see is altered. Not by my choice. I am tired of fighting this power around us, this power coming into our lungs, into our eyes and taking control. I will just drink even if it is the blood of my people."

Abyss-Dust Feet

"You fell asleep for the first time last night," My Girlfriend says, kissing me awake. "I guess you just needed to be home for a good night's rest. But please close your eyes next time. I've never witnessed someone sleeping with their eyes open, but it's terrifying."

I have wet the bed again. I am jittery and my still-Black is pale.

My Girlfriend pats my face. "What's wrong? You look shaken up."

She presses her palm to my forehead, then flicks her hand. "You're hot!"

Words refuse my mouth. When I sit up, the color doused on my skin has peeled off onto the bed covers, and it looks like the dead, wrinkled wings of a butterfly. My Girlfriend covers her mouth. She twists me around to look at my back. It looks like the skin of bone.

"We are bones now," I say. "We are turning into bones." My eyes are covered with the opaque film of sleep. I can't see well. The house is foggy, but certain parts of it are still surviving in my memory.

In the fall that morning, My Girlfriend stands in the ablution Brother designed. Worried, she stands me in the center where the ceiling opens into a great big circle, and she undresses and washes under the shower of the winter Sun. It splays itself on her body, and drains into the floor, a liquid gold, fusing the brown into her skin. I watch and feel something stir in me. Ecclesiastic light floods through the hole in the ceiling down her body. I kiss her and she kisses me back. The whole universe exists between us. For some time, perfect things do not evade us, but it does not last, for she leaves these words in my eyes, "Danger is coming. The Keeper of the Gate is remarked by you. It can't touch you, but it will figure a way to touch you. Once it touches you, you will be vulnerable."

"Is that a prophecy?" I ask, smiling and curling my hands through sunlight-wet Afro.

She twists with the air, the air is fluid; it is the undercurrent of water. My Girlfriend's mouth is a jarring wound, mouthing: "I am dreamskin."

I stumble back. *When did I fall asleep? I just came back,* I think.

"You chose to not sleep and invited us outside to join you," the wound with teeth in her face says. "Your insomnia strengthened us."

"Stay away from me." I fall onto my back.

The room is dreamskin. A body is naked. The bed has my body. A light treks through the dust in the room. Braids flit—the air carries them like water.

"You are asleep, but you are awake, too," My Girlfriend says, wearing dreamskin.

"No," I shout, running outside the house. I must leave this place. Dreamskin people will burn marks into my skin. I want them nowhere near me.

I run inside our residence to call Brother, but when we return outside, the girl who looked like me is gone and so is her tongue. I am gone. My tongue is gone. What stands there is a dog chewing on something. All I remember of that day is the neighbor screaming at me because my hands held the dog's mouth ajar as it whined. My sight turned to the space behind me, called by the feeling of being watched. I saw braids in their full length and still-Black arms unconnected to a body being dragged on the dusty ground around a corner. I ran toward it, but I found nothing. The braids looked like mine. The arms looked like mine. It was later I realized that the decapitated me began to haunt me since that day, trying to reclaim my body.

I stood in the street, the sun burning insanity into my skin until I collapsed.

***

During the night, my bladder full, I pass through a passage to empty myself. The silence in the corridor has a cold fog to its form. At the end of the corridor stands a white rooster. It stares at me, turns and walks away. I peek outside hoping the chicken coop wasn't left open. I damn Sister-In-Law hoping she didn't leave it open after she picked one for dinner.

I follow the rooster's path to the open door. I find myself, half-tranced in a dreamwalk, overlooking three women in the courtyard with the bones of a tree standing behind them. The night is a heavy, shadowed material that dresses their bodies with heavy fabrics to their feet, to their wrists. The fire makes the tree's deformed silhouette dance around itself for the silhouette bears the same shade as bark and night. I try to rub the crease of insomnia from my eyes, which is still dripping tears of dreams and nightmares. A metal tub stands in the center, gleaming light; the three women stand inside it, and in slow motion they cup the water and run it over their body, one after another until the water runs out of breath and volume. A cold liquid treads itself across my skin, threading itself into my bones, and snuffs the air from my lungs. My heart remains silent afraid to betray my presence to them.

The three women steer forward, their fabrics brush against every surface, a sweeping incantation against the ground, giving voice to an oft-muted air. They stand in the same manner as if a mirror reflects each unto the other, a pantomime. They look identical. The wind is colored by the smoke and its body is serpentine, refusing to dissolve into the air. It swivels, drawn back and forth by the women's voices, conjuring its movements. Don't look at the moon, the three women sing, it will hypnotize, lull your senses, your knees will knead the ocean until it has kneaded your breath into itself.

Their rooms overlook the courtyard, the plastic stripped off their windows; their living quarters have dark eyes. Something flickers inside their room. A shadow is dancing. Traditional beer brews in the near corner of the yard. Inside their rooms, the branches of a tree are burning. The smell is pungent, the fire grows. The rooms have quiet shadows that evoke the creature of solitude.

The widows do not talk, as if words are things they must not excrete. Beneath their abyss-dust feet, a folded leteise sits. They are wearing an outfit made from leteise, swung into night, swung to their dusted feet. The air has no breath, it carries their limbs like water. The metal tub shines so brightly that I can taste the sharp metal in my mouth. A girl with braids the length to her knees, covers her face except her lips, and whispers, "Ntlo e sule." I follow her outstretched finger: it points to our house. A baobab tree stands with one limb hanging a human torso, a human torso hung by its head full of long boxbraids, swaying in the air dusted with gravesand. It is My Girlfriend.

I return to my room and find My Girlfriend has sat up with her arms outstretched before her. "I look like water," she whispers. "I look like water." I am losing My Girl-friend. Her body used to be tinged by the sunset, a russet color.

First we turn into bones. Then we look like water.

I put her in the metal tub to contain her. I am losing sense. My Girlfriend is glass. I see through her. She is near-invisible, but she still feels herself more solid than stone. Her voice dwindles to a whisper. Soon I will be unable to hear her, to see her, to feel her. There is no reason for the train's existence when there will be no body to bury. The Shadow. They. Have found a solution. I gnash my teeth. The railway tracks will be destroyed. We will disappear from ourselves.

My language becomes sin washed from my mouth until I can't taste anything.

I stare at the floor. "They're not just destroying the railway tracks, they've put chemicals in our water. Soon we will have transitioned and assimilated into who they are or nothing."

"Shh, you still have a fever—you're sick. Your dreams are mingling with reality. The Keeper infected you. Please, you need to rest," My Girlfriend says.

"Grandma," I whisper. "My dreams are becoming worse."

***

I am unsleeping and the day walks into our room on hindfeet of light. The space beside me is empty. My Girlfriend is nowhere. I walk the hallways looking for her. The main door is ajar, and wind wheezes through the holes in the plastic windows. Silence is quieter today as I walk barefoot over the stones paving the path leading outside our yard. A white horse stands at the entrance of our gates, neighing and kicking out its feet.

I walk back into the house to find Brother waiting by the dining table for me.

"Our neighbors are selling," Brother says, holding a mug of coffee. "We should consider selling. The real estate market price for our house is high. We can find another plot of land and start afresh."

"So the same thing will happen?" I ask. "I am not moving."

"We can apply to transfer the house to another area," my brother says. "But it's more expensive than uprooting and starting again. We won't have enough money to be able to live in this home anymore. It's better to sell now and leave."

"We've lived here our entire lives."

"Developers have structured their idea in this area."

"What will be put here?"

"A luxury condo with mixed-use facilities," he says.

"We are being wiped out for luxury? We spent years building *our* luxury, building it for our family estate—it will be all wiped out?"

"It's not being wiped out," he says. "No one can control the earthquakes."

"The Shadow controls the earthquakes."

"Honestly, why do you listen to this foolish talk?"

"Did the city promise you something for you to consider selling *our* luxury?"

"I'm running a company to help sustain our lives," he says. "The only important lives are people and not buildings. What matters to me is that we have a place to sleep under, to have fun in, to eat in and to be safe in, even if the place we live in is under constant change."

"Your moralities are like a seesaw."

"Listen, we have been declining the city's offer for a year now," he says. "The longer we refuse to sell, the lower the value of the house goes. We'll have peanuts left."

"How can we remove that Keeper outside?" I ask. "It's destroying our lives. This thing that we speak—this new language—these words that burn our tongues, why must we speak this way? I miss the way we spoke."

"Accepting change is transitory as accepting its difficult nature; it will take time but you will come to terms with everything."

"Whatever you said makes no sense," I say. "Besides, no one is going to buy our house when it is marked by the widows. They aren't cleansed. They say our house is dirty with death."

"The city doesn't believe in that," Brother says. "The citizens in the districts are immune to superstition."

I return to my bedroom. My Girlfriend is against the window staring at the sky as if asking it to take her. I fetch our syrup of love and oil it around her tongue with my tongue. I wrap my arms around her. "If we don't leave, they'll taint the air to poison us with insanity. Our reality and dreams are mixed sometimes. We'll kill ourselves. We should just leave."

Decorations that should remain stuck to the walls are unfastened from their nails and fall to the floor. Someone is shaking our house. Our bedroom is a box of matchsticks, everything moves around like matchsticks caught in a whirl. All it needs is a catch to burn. I yank My Girlfriend, and we hide beneath the bed when the earthquakes thunder through our wards. There is no point in running outside: the earthquakes will be there, too. The only place they can't touch is the sky. A wall crumbles onto our bed. "I love you," My Girlfriend cries. "I will not die today," I say. "I refuse for us to die today." I grip her hand and pull her with me towards the entrance gates of our home. The Keepers of the Gate's fabric is in a fervor of delight. I run my hand through the debris of crumbled adobe wall and lodge it into the Keeper of our Gate's back. The piece of debris reflects off it and hits me in the stomach.

My Girlfriend bends over me and she is an angel smothered in hurt. "We have to leave or else we'll die!" she shouts. "We have to find safety." We walk down the path towards the gate. Sister-In-Law, baby wrapped to her back, comes screaming. "Your brother! Your brother! He's hurt!"

My Brother's body lies in the dusty street, covered in too much sun. The Keeper of our Gate leaves its station, walks toward my brother. The Keeper sways its heavy obsidian fabric back and forth, sweeping the dust from my brother's skin until he is bonelike. I scream to him. The molecules of air fibrillate and hold my voice away from him. The Keeper picks My Brother's body up. My Brother is loose and wrinkled, his face is expressionless. The Keeper picks My Brother's body up and wears him: the Keeper pushes its arm through his shoulder blade—my brother shrieks in pain—and it pushes another arm through the other shoulder blade until he folds out and it stands in his body. The Keeper is wearing my brother. It is wearing his legs, his arms, his strength.

The sun is a dull ring; it has burned a dull taste onto my tongue. I awake to my brother shaking sweat from my skin. "Stay away from me," I tell him. I push him away with beads of translucent things falling off my skin. I lock my doors and my knees and have beads that I count through my fingers. My sweat drops down like pebbles. My brother knocks and shakes the door handle.

"You are not my brother!" I shout.

The shadow that is reflected in the space below the door slowly retreats, but his form stands, still shaking the door. "Trust no man without a shadow," my grandmother used to say. "If shadows are felled from their owners it means the body is vacant of spirit. Something felled them."

I collapse onto my knees and reach out to his retreating shadow. I grasp a thread of his shadow. I twine it around my finger, pulling every thread of it toward me. It is all I have of My Brother. I will wrap it around my knitting needles and knit him whole.

My shadow wants to retreat, too, to flee, I tie myself around it, cold with sweat, my throat with the dull taste of castor oil. I jump into the metal table, hoping my shadow will remain an ocean I can immerse myself in. As I climb into the metal tub, a sharp piece that juts out catches my skin; my skin is a loose fabric, it tears open and I bleed the color from my skin. It drips onto the ground as I move. It is pouring out of me and I don't know how to contain the color coming off my skin.

"Help me," I pray to someone. Drops of brown paint the bottom of the metal tub. I press my finger to the droplets and smudge them against my wrist, but they evaporate to ash. I am disappearing. No train. No vain. I continue bleeding, drowning in the water of my shadow, in the ocean of my ethnicity. Rather I drown in it than in anything else.

"I don't want to die," I try to say, but the air refuses my voice. "I don't want to die."

Mercy is a pastor walking the hallways to pray for my sins, my existence. Mercy is a nun, caught in the cobweb of a dirge. My voice is being pulled like a string from my mouth. Someone keeps pulling and pulling it. My bones won't wake, won't fill out my arms to move. I have no power to stop it until I hear my voice coming from outside. Someone has my voice. Someone has my voice. They're Them singing with it, singing loud and proud. And a crowd, an audience claps, commands them for a voice they never clapped me for. Where is this audience coming from? Why do they accept a voice in a stranger who can't understand it? The Keeper wears my brother's body; the Keeper wears my voice.

I can't remember them. I can't remember the people I loved. Where are their names? I wake up; we are burning.

The Keeper wears my brother's body; the Keeper wears my voice.

My Brother is dead. My voice is dead.

Scent of Wilting Skin

Parts of me are juggled up, I feel amiss, out of place, but I'm back here now in this space trying to call back that spirit of calm and creativity, trying to paint with my breath, my lung the paintbrush of that world I wish for them to see, so they see it with the eye I use, not their eyes for their eyes suffer the poverty of sight: they are blind. I am nonsensical, words are too poor for my imagination. Hold me now, please.

We are back in our residence, My Girlfriend and I. A lone tree stands in the courtyard. It sways, dizzy from the wind. The night clocks are told by the rooster, we change into creatures of moonskin. We turn into bones. We turn into water.

"Your brother is gone, and so is the rest of your family," My Girlfriend says. "We don't have their bodies but we will treat it as if we do."

The Keeper wears my brother's body; the Keeper wears my voice.

My Girlfriend scrapes my hair off with a piece of sharp metal. The hair is part of the past and I watch it flake to the ground. Lightness settles in my chest. The death that surrounds the funeral accumulates into toxic dirt beneath my nailbeds; it is senyama. I wash the senyama from my skin to avoid it drifting off from my skin for our living-dead to inhale and suffer from. The fire flickers as it feeds on the hair shorn off from my skull and the clothes that belonged to my family; pieces of it flicker to the sky, and I watch it waver likes motes of my family. Tears leave my eyes and never return what feeling they take from me. My family is gone and I am not—but I am.

"People are boarding the train," she whispers. "We should, too."

"I. Am. Not. Leaving. My. Home."

A circular mirror sits in the ground, and I see the widow's reflection from last night, followed by their gestures. Except the mirror does not reflect them. It reflects the other side. In it the night is a material that is both thick and soft. It runs through my hands like viscous liquid. It's the third month today, and every mirror in our wards does not reflect us. When I look at myself, I see someone with moonskin. I wonder how I look. My Girlfriend appears now telling me that it is time, and I sense the inclemency of blindness. The older we age, the more our sight goes. I pace my hand along the motifs painted on the wall. Would these too be erased? What will replace them?

"There is no longer waking nor sleeping in this world," My Girlfriend says. We walk behind our residence, and take the same path my grandmother took when she was dead: towards the Train of the Dead.

"Where have you been," I try to ask, but there is no voice to my thoughts.

The train dissects our city, its rails creak each time it moves, it's like teeth scratching the night air for special offerings. As it stops on its platform, it collects the living who want to leave.

"See? People are leaving," My Girlfriend says.

Grandmother stands on the threshold, beckoning to

me, but I hold My Girlfriend back by her waist and tell her to never step foot on it or the air would refuse to fill her lungs. The train whips past us and it smells like the graveyard near the church grounds: the scent of wilting skin. I race behind it, searching each carriage hoping it will be absent of a family member. Each time I catch the solace in my grandmother's eyes, it brings my knees to the ground. No one offered my grandmother a seat. Hunched-back and wilting skin, she rests on her walking stick until it makes a hole through her chest straight out of her back. And you came by because you were worried about me. You took me outside. The sun was a solitude hand across the fields.

I am startled by a movement on my side: My Girlfriend. She utters, "You're still dreaming. Sepoko." An ancient word for people who still lack an understanding for those who left.

"If they want this land, then they must indulge in the things they call 'superstition,'" I whisper. "That is our army."

"What do you mean?"

"The dead on the train, the earthquakes, the ghosts, the widows—they want our land, they can have them as well."

"But how are we going to do that?" she asks.

"First their developments must be destroyed. Second they must fear this land so as to never step foot on it. The train is due for its arrival. The only way to evacuate them is to haunt them with our 'superstition'. We will start the earthquakes. The earth will swallow their evil. For now, we must wait for the death train."

"What if the earthquakes fail?"

"Then we get on the death train."

My body hurts

The clouds are crying. The air dry, crackling.

I have been thirsty for days. The water I drink does not quench. A streak of white slits the dark sky, the sun half-setting into the horizon. A loud crack, the snapping, breaking sky. No shatter to ground though. There is no sun. It is nighttime. Sun-bulbs are constellated along the streets, the pavements, the murram roads, the tarred roads. It is a silent, sleeping night.

It's been weeks since My Girlfriend and I have been living together. Another earthquake has come and gone. Another house has come and gone. Ward 5 has been replaced by a phallic-looking structure. Parts of the railway tracks are dismembering. We've tried fixing it, but it disperses again. The earthquake has left a chasm in the neighborhoods and markets. Our homes are down. We have to start rebuilding our lives again. My Girlfriend and I make it towards the wall by the districts, which in some way protects those from The Districts on the Other Side of the City from the train's death. Ours always crumbles down when we build it.

"We can't build a wall against our ancestors," My Girlfriend whispers, wearing a long-sleeved jersey in this humid heat. I stare at the only glove she's wearing. Odd.

"They're not ancestors," I repeat my brother's words. We sit on the wall overlooking the districts, watching all the houses safe in their yards, safe in their land, safe in their sky, and wonder what it feels like to be safe. The Shadow is a solid thickness in the air, translucent, but not permeable by people—specifically us. We can't ever break into the districts.

My Girlfriend has a mellow look in her eyes that makes one want to pray. "The earthquake is going to shake the sky one day and the stars will fall down and burn our land."

"But the sky belongs to everyone," I say.

"It doesn't." Her jaw tenses as she notices something in The District on the Other Side of the City. "The building material...I recognize it. It's the same as the one in your house."

I look at every structure that swallows everything in its presence. Everything is shiny and magnifies the sun's hold. It hurts my eyes to look. The glare, the reflection, the greyness of it all blinds the trees that they have begun to fade.

"They have already started the rehabilitation of our buildings," she says. "Everything in our wards is changing."

"The construction is only going to take place in the fields by the railway tracks," I say. "It's empty land that no one uses, yet. That's the first stage of the city development."

The air expands into coolness as a mass shuttle of raindrops jet from their station of clouds. We hop up, giggling and push-playing each other, yelping "Pula!"

"See who can balance better. I'm a tight-rope walker." She is a bird, arms outstretched, an airplane in the midst of mundanity. She is a sleek blade traversing the slim top of the wall, gingerly stepping over the sun-bulbs propped onto the wall. One step after another. I look down, the ground below folds in and out of my vision. I close my eyes, take a deep breath, nausea thick and puffy as cotton in my mouth. The base of my spine tingles with sweat. "Hey, help, feel faint," I try, but the wind snatches the words from my mouth and chunks them far away from My Girlfriend.

She's widened the gap between us.

Don't look down. Don't look down. The wind sways her from the sides, grabs her side with claws to take her down.

"Be careful!" I reach out, only grasping the loose fragment of her scent, wavering in the wind.

She turns her head, her straight-set teeth spark with laughter. "Come on. You'll be a'ight." The wind jitters about her, shaking her clothes about, a tornado encircling her. I'm still on my fours trying to balance myself. Too late. The sun-bulb cracks, a sizzle of smoke astonishes the air, shards scar its skin, the air whines down into empty black.

Her scream punctures the night apart.

The dark eclipses my sight, I lose my balance, scrape my arm against the abrasive brick surface as gravity drags me down. I am a meteor; the ground punches my face. Earth and pebbles fill my mouth. I sit up, groaning, wiping dirt and hurt from my bruised face. I can't see. I can't see! The dark has covered my eyes with its hands. I flail around. Pain fires up and down my arms. The sun! Where's the sun!

My Girlfriend's screams hold my body up, maneuver me through the dark mist toward her, until my foot feels her body first. The sun-bulbs flare. It was a power outage. The air exhales with the last fall of rain. She holds her knee to her chest, her foot soaking in the muddy water. I yank off my coat and wrap it around her, guide her toward the train station shelter.

I scream when I look down. Her…her foot is gone. Cleanly sliced off.

My body hurts. My body hurts. Pull yourself together.

"My foot," she cries. "My foot."

I bow down before her, inspect her leg. There's no blood. There's no blood. Her foot is gone. Dismembered. "I'm going to pull your pants leg up, okay?" I look across the tracks hoping to see her foot. I need to take her to the hospital, to the traditional doctor. What am I supposed to do? I fold back the fabric, the amputation reveals no broken-off bone or nerves and tissue, it's brown, smooth as skin. She's no longer screaming. In fact, she's seated up staring at me. Just staring at me. She stands—*no, don't, the hospital, we have to go,* I say—she stands as if on both feet, but the other's gone. I stare back, mouth gaping. The sun-bulb lights surround her form with a bright halo. She points blankly at my exposed arms. Where the raindrops touched my skin are constellations of transparency, the spots like telescopes to the other side, sending sharp pinpoints of light through me.

"What is wrong with me?" I shout, trying to flee from my skin. "What's wrong with us?"

"What's wrong with *them*," she corrects me, staring at the wall that separates the two parts of the city. "It's the districts' doing. Pain. A notification, not of bone fracture but of erasure."

I rock myself back and forth. The pain I felt from earlier wasn't from the fall, it was from the rain, scorching my arms with… "Pain is a notification of what?"

"They're decapitating us with erasure, rain their tool." Her face is a stern blade of anger. "We're already disappearing. They're not just building on our land, they're building erasure onto our skin. Such bad guys, such heavy artillery. They're closing in on us. Low blow."

"Now it's my foot. What's next? They're decapitating

me bit by bit," she continues.

"But...we can't just disappear. Where will we go to?" I shake my head. "No, what if it's not the districts' doing? What if this is how the missing people disappear? What if we're becoming Translucent?" I look about me. "I don't know what to trust. Can we trust the air? Who's the enemy?"

She laughs, but it's not a happy sound. "Spirits have more existence than us. I can see a spirit better than I can see myself. The dead are already safe. If we can't join them, we have no home on this land, we have no home in the land of the dead." She looks at the districts again, and this time a sad wind wipes her tear away. "They are destroying everything. I told you: Danger stands in every doorway. It doesn't have to be loud as a bomb or a gunshot. It has the feet of silence."

When I look down, I scream. "Your whole leg has disappeared!"

My Girlfriend is smiling. "The train. I can hear it. It will be here shortly."

Slowly her waist is disappearing.

"Just stay with me for these last minutes. I want to remember this when I'm dead," she says. "Stop fighting it."

The darkness is filled with the Keeper of the Gates, watching her death. Their arms raised toward us. She falls to the ground. "I'm sleepy," she whispers.

"Stay awake, please stay awake." Half her body remains in my arms. My tears splatter her face.

"Just hold me," she slurs. The death train needs to get here now. I need to get her onto the death train before she disappears. We need to get onto the train.

The Keeper of our Gate pushes The Shadow into our huddled space. Every civilian is lying on the ground, except some...who were touched by Dreamskin. They're huddled by their families' sleeping bodies, crying. I try communicating with the Keeper of the Gates. Again and again. I plead to it for help, stupidly thinking it will help. My throat throws up my own language in italic forms into the air. The pain welds itself into my stomach. My Girlfriend lies on the ground with black shiny eyes. The Keeper of our Gate raises its formless arm, catching my words, changing their letters and throws it back into my face like dice, so they transform into new sentences in my mind: *your language does not fit this market, does not fit this society.* Those words must be what it tells me. My Girlfriend's eyes are liquid black and they melt down her face.

It raises its hands. The first time I hear it speak: *Rain.* Water falls from the skies in torrents and violence.

The Keeper of our Gate holds me down without touching me. Nulls my screaming. Something tears into me without touching me. It performs surgery on me, and the words are gone, the memory is vacant, and I can't remember who I am. *Now you are suitable for society, for the market.* I stare at my arms and touch myself expecting blood and holes, but there's no physical evidence of what the figure did. When I look across the street, I see another me whom I can see through. This me is broken, not straight, her bones jut out, her mouth is laid with flies and her tongue lies on the ground, bloody and twitching. The Keeper of our Gate stands watching. The cold fog evaporating from their black cloth is perfumed with elation.

I'm dense with hysteria. I stretch my hand to the remaining lips of My Girlfriend. The air has devoured My Girlfriend. She is gone. She is dead. My scream is a sword into the clouds. They murdered every bit of me. I will murder what they know. In the distance, the time of to-morrow, the Sun begins to bleed. The horizon absorbs her blood, but soon it will overflow. Soon everything will overflow with the solitude dragging of Danger's feet into our oval mouths. The war has started.

You Were Still Alive Inside Your Mother's Womb When They Decided to Kill You

My Girlfriend was born on the train. The week after her mother died.

I know. You've been eager to hear this ever since I started telling you everything you can't remember. I mentioned it once and I'm surprised you didn't bug me to elaborate it. It was hard for me to reiterate what happened to My Girlfriend; it presses trauma to my bones, makes me live through the experience. She suffered. *You* suffered a great deal. I should be happy you don't remember, but the memory you gave me torments me—I don't know why you'd want it back.

You were still alive inside your mother's womb when they decided to kill you.

I can never reveal it without feeling nauseous. See, her mother wasn't ready for a child and sought someone to snuff its existence. It is a terrible thing to recall this, it sends my body into spasms. The body parts were severed as they were one-by-one pulled from her mother's vagina: the legs, the abdomen, the head crushed so as to ease its exit from her. After that, the rest of My Girlfriend's home was sucked out, as if she never lived in it. The fetus lived through the abortion three times. My Girlfriend survived through that three times. It pains me to imagine what torture she lived through before she was born, how she fought to survive, how she was forced to survive, to live through it to sustain a stupid law, a law breathed by our culture to not terminate pregnancy. That experience lived in her mind, it lived in her actions, in her memories—she always woke up screaming, remembering the tearing off of her limbs.

The first three attempts had the fetus extracted and buried. Each time it failed, they exhumed the burials and found nothing but earth and plants. Not one limb of you was found. They knew then that her body was not compatible for aborting. They knew it is a law by the ancestors. A law that cannot be defeated, yet they tried.

I am so sorry, love. I am so sorry. Please don't cry. When you were born on the Train of the Dead you couldn't consume what the dead consumed. You were given to your uncle and you stayed with him until you found a way to pay for your living.

Most citizens' noses couldn't detect what language her scent spoke. Her thoughts painted the air amber and had a peculiar scent to them. You could always tell where she had been in the house from their trail, from what she was thinking. The scent was putrid and stronger when her thoughts were erratic and burning with doubt and confusion. Those, unable to read her thoughts or the language of her scent called her smelly and threw powders of soap at her. When happy, her thoughts perfumed the air with pure intoxication that flowers bloomed and wilted in one swift moment. She tried to stop thinking. She tried to cover herself up.

She tried to skin herself. In the end, she couldn't erase herself from herself.

"We have no sovereign rule to anything, not even the life in our bones," My Girlfriend said once.

I wanted to give her hope, but I couldn't grow it in the garden.

I. Am. Burning.

I can't remember them. I can't remember the people I loved. Where are their names? I wake up; we are burning.

We are invisible, more opaque than spirits, but we still exist. No one sees us, no one hears us. The cubicle glass is a magnifying glass through which the sun goes through. This cubicle sits on stilts. It's a machine for living. We walk through the city streets, the places that we used to call home, painted the color of air. They walk through us, they inhale us, they yawn their comfort in our invisible forms. This is not home anymore. My body is not home anymore. I can't switch off the pain—it is a sun in the sky, always burning. The language that was a tenant of this place can no longer call this home. It is buried in Nowhere, a place without mention, without a signal, without a connect. But I saw Language one day, sitting in their home, looking nervous and scared and so tight to itself as if avoiding inhaling too much space. Sometimes I see Language as a toy that a kid kicks through what used to be our streets. Sometimes I see Language smashed continuously by some-one's teeth. Sometimes Language is burning in the fireplace or being ogled at in a window-cased box. But the one place I never saw Language in is my throat, my vocal chords, my ears. I can't remember how my voice used to give birth to it. I can remember how Language felt when it passed through my lips. Pieces of us are scattered everywhere, and my pain is bleeding in every crevice it finds. I'm still searching for a god who will allow my skin. Please come now. Please break this glass cubicle. Take my bones at least. Give them rest. Give them home. Here I am: I am burning. Of all things, death refuses me. Here. I. Am. Burning.

My skin wilts silently, fluttering by like a flower's petals. The Keeper wears my brother's body; the Keeper wears my voice. I wear my soul.

Hope is my warrior. They didn't believe in the earth-quakes, our dreamskin, the ghosts haunting this place, the train. If it affects them, it could scare them off. "If we work together, we can call on the train, the train will call on the earthquake. They don't know the rules. The ghosts will wreck them. The dreamskin will scare them. With casualties, there'll be dreamskin everywhere."

The wail of the train announces it arrival.

I leap onto the wall that separates the two parts of the city.

The tracks rattle, metal groaning against metal.

I will fight the death wrapped around my name. I will step onto the train and become who we are. It is a lie, being near the dead doesn't destroy us, it wakes us up, makes us alive.

I am not crazy.

I am not crazy.

I am not crazy. "You want our land, you'll take our problems!" I dig my hands into the earth. "Earthquake!" Shrapnel slithers through the ground, the tall-knife struc-ture buckles—the façade is patchworked in diamond-shaped metal pieces that buckle at the edges—it creaks, shoots out every piece of its face.

I scream to the sky. "That's your weapon there, spitting out large pieces of bullets!" They bump into the ghost-like dead ones, one starts chewing on their legs. "You're not supposed to touch them. Respect their space. You didn't believe in our train, in our dead, in our earthquakes. Here's your land!" The world groans, the world shatters, their chess pieces fall into the chasm, the mouths of the angry earth.

I am Translucent. We are alive.

450 Suns Later

The graveyard is open today. All day.

I walk, run, fly toward the train station. She is there. In the third carriage.

She turns around dazed, My Girlfriend. The sunlight is a miracle around her form. I can still tell the color of her eyes: a flicker of brown. I can still tell the millions of coils holding steadfast to her head. I can still tell the dark brown gripping her bones with fear. I can still tell who she is.

My Girlfriend stands in her birthplace, the train where her mother died giving birth. There is shadow to her spirit. There is smile to her teeth. She is not vacant of holiness. She is fluffed from evil. The train glitters under the sun and moon in the womb of blue sky. Down the steel steps, she goes. She kneels before me, presses her head into my thighs. "I still love you. Do you believe that? Can that just be enough for you?" Her light brown eyes shimmer with tears.

I wipe her tears and kiss her cheek. "Our love is not a mirage on the horizon. It is here. It will always be here…"

The train takes my family and my lovers to and fro the abyss. They live part-time in ancestral land, they live part-time here. My ex-boyfriend is my husband. My Girlfriend is my wife, my first partner on the hierarchy, my husband the second; he follows the first partner's orders. Our family name is Mohumagadi.

My Girlfriend smiles. "I have a name. I have skin-color stitched with the ethnicity of my tribe."

My family step down from the train, still-Black. Always still-Black. Their skin-color is stilled to their bones. Mirrors in every smile, every speech, every tone. They are still here, they are still a part of us. We are near the dead. We are sacred.

With war, there is blood, there is irrevocable death. We live through dimensions, we love through dimensions. She is dead. I am alive. We are lovers.

Acknowledgments

Firstly, thank you to the super-awesome Michael Takeda who saw something in this novella to offer publication. Many thanks goes to the Pink Narcissus Press team, Duncan Eagleson for the cover design and to Josie Brown for her superb editing. Thank you to everyone who supported me with my writing—friends and family. Thank you to Aubrey for reading early drafts of this novella and offering your comments. Also thank you to my writing critique buddies, past and present, who've helped me evolve as a writer—Cheryl Ntumy, Sharon Tshipa, Jen Finelli, Steven Hanton, Tshetsana Senau, Virginia Harrington. Thank you to my crazy but awesome and hilarious friends/family: Boitumelo, Omphile, and Lesego. I much appreciate the following mentorships that provided me with such invaluable lessons: Justina Ireland's *Writing In The Margins* and Kate Brauning's *Breakthrough Writers' Boot Camp* program. Thank you to my writing mentor F.K Omoregie (R.I.P.), who read my terrible stories and offered me advice to be a better writer. And thank you to you reader for picking up this book.

About the Author

Tlotlo Tsamaase is a Motswana writer of fiction, poetry, and architectural articles. Her work has appeared or is forthcoming in the *Prisms* anthology, *Terraform*, *Apex Magazine*, *Strange Horizons*, *Wasafiri*, *Botswana Women Write*, and other publications. Her poem "I Will Be Your Grave" is a Rhysling Award nominee. Her short story, "Virtual Snapshots" was longlisted for the 2017 Nommo Awards. Tlotlo Tsamaase works and lives in Botswana. Find her online at www.tlotlotsamaase.com

OTHER BOOKS AVAILABLE FROM
PINK NARCISSUS PRESS

SUSPENDED HEART
Magic realism stories by Heather Fowler
"Fowler possesses a relatively bright and affectionate vision of mystical worlds, and this "collector's edition with bonus stories' [...] reads a bit like the late, great Carol Emshwiller — funny chronicles of fantastic events in the lives of unextraordinary people." *– The New York Times Book Review*
ISBN: 978-1-939056-15-3

THE KNIFE'S DAUGHTER
A Korean fairy tale by Andrew Coletti
"Coletti's debut cleverly explores how themes of gender fluidity and reluctant adherence to duty cast new light on the classic fantasy quest story. [...] This is a perfect excursion for readers interested in examining how others' expectations can be far more challenging and dangerous than dragons or evil sorcerers." — *Publishers Weekly, *starred review**
ISBN: 978-1-939056-14-6

THE RAMSHEAD ALGORITHM
Fantastical stories by KJ Kabza
"KJ Kabza seems to specialize in altered states, dream states, and has a range from flights of fancy to gut-wrenching terror... You will treasure this collection. RECOMMENDED." *—Abyss & Apex*
ISBN: 978-1-939056-13-9

CPSIA information can be obtained
at www.ICGtesting.com
Printed in the USA
LVHW021926130521
687357LV00014B/1311